Somewhere Along the Way

The Andrades

Ruth Cardello

Author Contact

website: RuthCardello.com
email: ruthcardello@gmail.com
Facebook: Author Ruth Cardello
Twitter: RuthieCardello

Luke Andrade:

Wealthy, talented, fiercely loyal. He's the glue that holds his family together, but every man has a breaking point. When he heads to Ohio to attend a funeral, he does so with the intention of taking time off to clear his head. The very last thing he expects to do is meet a woman.

Cassie Daiver:

Scarred, but not broken. She's recreating herself in a small town far away from her painful childhood.

He's angry with the world and himself. She finally has something she's afraid to lose. They couldn't have met at a worse time.

Luke and Cassie are about to discover love often happens somewhere along the way, and usually, when one least expects it.

Sign up for Ruth's Mailing List

ruthcardello.com/signup

One random newsletter subscriber will be chosen every month in 2015. The chosen subscriber will receive a $100 eGift Card! Sign up today by clicking on the link above!

Copyright

Dedication

To all of the lovely women in Defiance, Ohio, who welcomed me so warmly when I flew out there to meet their book club. Although the people and places in Somewhere Along the Way are purely fictional, I hope I captured the essence of your small-town warmth and sense of community.

Defiance is a great place to fall in love.

Chapter One

(Before you start reading, consder signing up for Ruth Cardello's newsletter. Don't miss a release or sale.)
forms.aweber.com/form/58/1378607658.htm

CASSIE DAIVER KNELT on the cushioned bench in front of the casket. She lowered her eyes to her folded hands and took a deep, fortifying breath.

What a way to finally meet, Emma.

I don't know what happens to us after we die, but I hope you can hear me.

Thank you. That's primarily what I came here to say. Thank you for being the kind of person a whole town could love—so much so they wanted the best for you even after you moved to New York.

It doesn't feel like two years could have passed since I saw you on the news. I remember exactly where I was, though. I was working a double shift at the sandwich shop near the tenement I grew up in—feeling trapped and helpless. Then I heard your voice. It didn't matter that you were talking about going through something no one your age should have to. There was a hope in your tone, a refusal to give up, that stopped me in my

1

tracks.

I dropped an overflowing cup of coffee and turned to watch you describe how you had gone to the East Coast in search of a cure and stayed partly because you fell in love with the area. You were a beacon of positive energy, even in what must have been a dark time for you. Your strength made me see I hadn't fought hard enough for my own life.

I won't bore you with the details. You're probably busy doing whatever people do when they cross over, but I needed to tell you I wish you'd found your cure.

I wish we could have had this conversation in person. I considered contacting you—about a hundred times. I didn't know how to thank you for giving me hope.

For showing me there are places filled with good people. I didn't have to settle for what I grew up in.

Cassie gripped the velvet-covered armrest. *Can I tell you something I haven't announced to anyone yet?* Cassie closed her eyes for a moment. *It's not like you can spill the secret. Oh, my God, I'm babbling. Sorry, that joke was in poor taste. I say stupid things when I get nervous.*

Breathe.

Cassie slipped a hand into the pocket of her coat and lovingly pulled out an envelope that contained a photo of a man. *I also had a selfish reason for coming to see you today. Meet sperm donor #57. Two unsuccessful cycles of IUI so far. This is his last chance before I try fertility drugs, another donor, or go more invasive with the methods. It could be a year before I can afford something like that.*

If you have any pull over there, can you put in a good word for me? I really want a baby. Blinking back tears, Cassie bowed her head. *I've heard women talk like that before, and I always thought they were crazy. But here I am, begging whoever is listening to help me start my family.*

Even though we never met, you guided me to a better place. Is it wrong to ask you to help me one last time?

I've made a stable life for myself here.

And I have so much love to give.

A woman in line behind Cassie cleared her throat. Cassie glanced over her shoulder and realized there was a long line of people waiting for her to move on. She looked down at the peaceful expression on the woman in the casket.

I should go. Thank you for listening.

I will always be grateful that our paths crossed, even if distantly. Tell everyone in heaven you made a difference. I hope one day to be able to say the same.

Cassie stood and wiped tears from her cheeks. She gave her condolences to each family member in line after the casket. If some of them knew she'd never met Emma, they didn't say. They shook her hand warmly and seemed pleased when Cassie described how Emma had inspired her.

Cassie was making her way to the exit of the funeral home, lost in her thoughts, when she walked into a tall wall of muscle. She mumbled, "Excuse me," and took a step aside without looking up. Her emotions were raw, and her stomach churned with nerves. She stumbled.

Two strong hands steadied her. "Are you okay?"

With tears still blurring her vision, Cassie nodded automatically and pulled away from the man. "Yes, sorry."

"Did you know her well?" the man asked softly in a deep, cultured voice.

It was only then that Cassie looked up at him. Although she'd never seen him in town, he felt familiar. She frowned. It didn't matter. "No, but she's why I'm here."

"Me, too," he said simply.

The pain and yearning in his eyes called out to Cassie. Shook her. His eyes were dark and tormented. Who was he? His expensive suit and perfectly trimmed jet-black hair implied wealth at a level above anyone in town. Emma had been single and had lived in New York City for a long time. Was he a lover of hers, there to pay his respects to her family?

If so, Emma, you had good taste. It was hard not to appreciate the man's broad shoulders, his imposing height, and the deliciously toned abs Cassie had brushed against.

What is wrong with me? I'm at a funeral.

And I could already be pregnant.

Without saying another word, Cassie stepped around the man and hastily exited the funeral home. She walked through the parking lot without looking back. The cold winter air bit at her bare hands as she unlocked her car.

Like someone leaving the scene of a crime, she drove off and raced back to the bed and breakfast she owned. It was only after she had donned her apron and was kneading bread dough that she began to relax.

Everything was going to work out. She simply had to stay focused. Luckily she had several hours of baking to occupy her thoughts that night. Money had been tight when she'd first purchased the bed and breakfast, Home Sweet

Home, and she'd brought in extra money by baking cup-cakes, sweets, and breads for some of the local restaurants. She'd named her side business, Cassie's Creations. Perhaps not the most creative, but people seemed to like it.

She wondered where Mr. Expensive Suit had chosen to spend the night. He looked like someone who would rent a suite at one of the posh hotels in Toledo.

Forget him. He's probably already flying back to wherever he came from.

"So, I'll be staying at my son's tonight," a cranky female voice said from the doorway of the kitchen.

Cassie kept kneading the dough without looking up. "Should I expect you back tomorrow?"

"Not if this storm gets worse. I don't know if I like the idea of you staying here, either. Why don't you come home with me?"

Cassie looked up then and smiled gently. "You know I have to bake for tomorrow."

Matilda Cameron buttoned the front of her coat and gave her short gray hair a pat. "Who's going to pick up their orders in a blizzard?"

"It's just a little snow, Tilly."

"My old bones don't lie. The weatherman will be calling it a blizzard by the time we set our heads down on our pillows tonight."

Cassie began to knead the dough again with determina-tion. "I'll be fine. Besides, if the airports close, who knows, I may get guests tonight."

"And what am I?" the older woman asked with a harrumph.

Cassie smiled gently. "A friend."

"I offered to pay you."

"Tilly, I can't take your money. You live down the street."

"You're too proud. Trust me, it would be worth every penny. You don't know what it's like over there. The older I get, the bossier my son becomes. Now he doesn't think I should drive. He took my keys. Can you believe that? What's he going to do next? Ground me for missing curfew?"

"Didn't you run over Mr. Landry's mailbox twice this month?"

Tilly pulled her knit hat down low on her head and glowered at Cassie. "If someone keeps crashing into his mailbox, you'd think he'd realize it's poorly placed. No, instead he just ratfinks me out to Jimmy."

"You're lucky Mr. Landry has a crush on you, or he'd be calling the police instead of your family."

Tilly blushed. "Crush? What nonsense. Besides, he's too young for me."

"He's seventy-six."

"And I'm eighty. I was out of high school by the time Myron started shaving."

Cassie held back a chuckle. There was no denying Mr. Landry had carried a torch for Tilly most of his life. It was sweet and a little sad at the same time. Why some things came easily for people, while others waited and yearned, was a topic too close to another subject she was trying not to think about. "You're right, the town would label you a cougar in no time. Your reputation would be shot."

Tilly cocked her head to one side while resting a hand on the door handle behind her. "You're lucky I like you, Cassie. Should I have my son bring by some firewood?"

Suddenly serious, Cassie shook her head. "You don't have to do that. I have plenty. Do you want me to walk you home?"

"Nah, Jimmy's coming to get me. You sure you don't want to stay with us?"

Raising her chin, Cassie placed the dough into a bowl and covered it with a towel. "Thanks, Tilly, but I'm fine."

More than fine.

I'm home.

✧   ✧   ✧

"DR. ANDRADE."

Luke turned away from the door he'd been staring at absently. An image of the beautiful brunette who had literally run into him lingered in his mind. Although they'd barely said more than a few words to each other, he'd fought an irrational desire to chase after her. There was something about her . . .

When she'd looked up at him, he'd almost forgotten why he'd come to Ohio. The hum of subdued conversations around them had disappeared. For just a sliver of time, it had felt as if she were the reason he was there. Those dark brown eyes—beautiful even through the tears. The encounter had felt inexplicably important.

Luke shook his head to clear it. He was drawn back to

the reality of his trip by the short, older woman who had taken his hand in hers. "You came."

Smiling warmly down at Beverly Turner, Luke reminded himself this was the reason—the only reason—he'd come. "Did you doubt I would?"

Emotion gave a shine to Beverly's eyes as she shook her head. "No. Emma spoke of you often. It was kind of you to stay in touch with her even after she was no longer your patient."

Luke bowed his head at the memory. "I'd like to think we were friends."

A quiet moment passed.

Beverly said, "You missed Dr. Andrews. He came by this morning to beat the storm. He mentioned you took the news of Emma's passing hard."

Luke wanted to look away, hide his pain, but he didn't. He couldn't give Beverly her daughter back, but he could give her something. "Your daughter touched more lives than you'll likely ever know. I try not to get too involved in the lives of my patients, but Emma wouldn't allow that. She met me several times before and after the surgery. I swear if she could have talked to me during her actual operation she would have."

Beverly gave a teary smile. "She always did like meeting new people."

Luke smiled. "She didn't hold back her opinions either."

"That's for sure." With a soft laugh at the memory, Beverly nodded. She let go of his hand and glanced around. "You do realize every woman here checked her makeup when you walked in, don't you? We don't get many single doctors passing through. You are still single, aren't you, Dr. Andrade?"

Luke winked down at Beverly. "Only because your husband found you first."

Beverly laughed, tucked a salt-and-pepper curl behind her ear, and blushed. "You're so bad, but I can see why Emma adored you." Her face sobered, and she said, "I called the hospital to settle our bill with them, and they said it had been paid in full. Emma had a private room and the best doctors in the country consulting on her case. Someone was very generous to my family."

Luke ducked his head and looked away. "I'm not surprised. Whoever did that was likely inspired by her in the same way I was."

Beverly laid a hand on Luke's arm. "We know it was you."

Luke placed a hand warmly over hers. "I only wish I could have done more."

A tall, older man came up beside Beverly and placed an arm around her waist, while warmly offering a hand to Luke in greeting. "Dr. Andrade. Thank you for coming. It means a lot to our family that you flew out here."

Luke shook the hand of Emma's father. "Your daughter will be missed, sir. She touched a lot of lives."

Quinn Turner's lips thinned, and his face tightened with emotion. "She did. There was a woman here earlier who said the same thing. She'd never actually met Emma, but she said my daughter was the reason she'd moved to Defiance. She said Emma and our town gave her hope when she needed it."

Luke glanced over his shoulder at the door, wondering if the woman Quinn was referring to could be the same woman he couldn't stop thinking about. Luke forced himself to focus on Emma's father. "I don't doubt it. I remember the first time I met your family. I had never had a consult with an entire clan in attendance."

Beverly hugged her husband and smiled up at him. "The town had had a fundraiser, remember? They raised enough to send us all to New York."

Quinn smiled gently down at his wife. "I remember. The story made the news. We hated the attention at the time, but when I heard that woman talking about Emma like she was an angel sent to save her, I knew it had all happened for a reason."

Beverly tapped her chin in thought. "I spoke to her, too. Cassandra Daiver, I believe she said. She bought the old bed and breakfast on the west side of town a few years ago."

Quinn frowned. "I remember now. I wonder how it's working out for her?"

Beverly shrugged. "We've been away so much, I feel out of touch with what's going on in our own town. I hope she's doing well."

Quinn nodded. "When everything settles down again, let's check in on her. I think Emma would want us to. Ms. Daiver looked like a woman who could use a friend."

Luke excused himself from the conversation and moved to the other side of the room. It didn't feel right to want to know about Cassandra more than to speak with the rest of

Emma's family. Although he and Emma had only ever been friends, she and the town she'd come from had been a reminder of the good in the world. In the two years Luke had known her, Emma hadn't been angry about the cancer that had spread through her body. She'd surrounded herself with positive people and continued to live her life joyfully, spreading inspiration to others who crossed her path.

Emma had often said there was good in every situation and every person, if you kept your heart open to it.

She wouldn't be pleased with him if she knew he was beginning to believe she'd been wrong. Luke rubbed his hands over his face. It had been because of Emma's unwavering faith in humanity that he had gone to see his ailing mother, despite receiving word she didn't want visitors.

Patrice Andrade had been sitting in her parlor when Luke had barged past her house staff. He'd needed to see the state of her health with his own eyes. She looked significantly older, even though it had been only a month or so since he'd last visited her. She'd ordered him to leave. He'd implored her to listen to him.

Even when a member of her house staff had come to stand beside him, Luke hadn't given up. He'd begged his mother to give him access to her medical records.

Patrice had risen to her feet and approached Luke. Her softly coifed hair was a harsh contrast to the bitterness that twisted her features. "Look at you. You always were pathetic. Like a dog that comes back no matter how many times I kick it. Weak. Just like your father. I don't want you here. I don't need your help. The sight of you sickens me."

Although Luke had witnessed his mother's foul temper since childhood, he'd never seen such unveiled ugliness. He told himself it was likely a type of dementia setting in during her illness, but he was sadly familiar with that coldness in her eyes. He'd briefly met the eyes of her butler. The compassion he'd seen there had only made him feel worse.

His brothers had tried to convince him that beneath their mother's manipulative, harsh exterior there was only bitterness and resentment toward her sons. Luke had never allowed himself to believe them, but her words echoed through him—even here at a funeral.

I'm not my father, a man who hid a family in Venice rather than have the courage to divorce a woman he didn't love.

As Luke watched the line of mourners pay their respects and move on to speak with Emma's family, he acknowledged another reason he'd felt compelled to come to this town regardless of the impending weather.

He was searching for something. He hated the consuming anger he felt each time he thought of his mother. A doctor dedicates his life to saving people. Luke couldn't justify feeling the planet might be better off without his mother.

So far all he'd found were more questions. What kind of son wondered why good people like Emma were taken early while his vile mother remained?

What did he want to find in Defiance? Hope? Evidence of good in the world? Acceptance and concern were etched in the kind faces of the friends and family who had gathered for Emma.

Emma, I resent my mother as much as my brothers do.
What if I am like my father—a fraud?

He hadn't spoken to Emma in the last month, and he regretted that. All three of his brothers seemed to be getting along, and that should have made Luke happy, but he'd lost his ability to believe it would last.

Signs that it wouldn't were already appearing.

Just a few days ago, fresh from hearing about Emma's passing, Luke had received a phone call from his cousin, Maddy. She'd sounded upset about something she'd uncovered about the family. He and Maddy had always been close. She had a big heart, and like him, had always fought to keep the family together.

Lately though, she'd become obsessed with uncovering old family secrets. She'd claimed only the truth had the power to heal whatever had caused a rift between his mother and the rest of the Andrade clan. He'd warned her to leave it alone.

When it came to his family, nothing good came from asking questions. Maddy had wanted to meet with him so she could show him what she'd uncovered. In an act that had been entirely out of character, Luke had refused and hung up on her.

He was done.

He was tired of pretending to be the perfect son, the perfect brother, the perfect cousin.

He'd cleared his schedule and told his office he was taking an extended vacation somewhere far from New York. Emma's death had shaken him. He hadn't been her primary doctor. Still, he couldn't stop thinking he should have stayed more involved. Pushed her to get more testing, more opinions.

Her death and his mother's obvious declining health were situations where he felt powerless. It wasn't a feeling he was accustomed to. Nor was the anger that curled his hands into fists at the thought of either.

He needed a break, and he was taking one. As soon as he left the funeral home, he was heading back to the airport. He intended to book the first flight he found to anywhere warm. A week of sun might lift his mood.

Emma, do you remember making me promise I'd visit your town? I should have come while you were here to give me a tour. What was it you wanted me to see?

The lights in the funeral home flickered. A member of Emma's family stepped up to a podium and said, "Thank you all for coming tonight. We just received news that the storm has worsened. They say there will soon be blizzard conditions, so we're calling off the gathering at the hall. Go home. Take care of your families. Thank you again for coming out in the snow, and please drive carefully."

Luke took out his phone and searched the closest airport for flight information. All outgoing flights had been canceled. He turned to the man at his side and said, "What's the nearest hotel?"

"There are a few just north of town, but if the roads are as bad as they say, you'd be better off staying with someone in town." The man held up a hand as a thought came to him. "Or at that bed and breakfast—Home Sweet Home.

It's only a couple blocks from here. I bet there are vacancies this time of year."

"Is that the one owned by . . .?"

"It was bought by a woman from Detroit. Kathy Deider or something like that."

"Cassandra Daiver?"

"Yes, that's who owns it. You should try that place. A cousin of mine stayed there. He said the place had been renovated, and the food was great. I hear the owner is quite the looker, too, but she might not be into men because my cousin said she gave him quite the brush-off when he asked her out."

Luke's heart started beating double time in his chest. "Thanks for the heads-up."

Quinn and Beverly crossed the room to Luke. "Dr. Andrade, do you need a place to stay?"

Luke shook his head. He shook Quinn's hand and gave Beverly a hug. "I found a place in town."

Beverly looked up at him. "Are you sure? We have plenty of room."

"I'm sure." The last thing Luke wanted to do was spend the night with Emma's family. He used the excuse of wanting to speak to a few other family members to extricate himself from Beverly and Quinn.

After making his way through the quickly deepening snow in the parking lot, Luke found the number of the bed and breakfast on his phone and called it. He didn't realize he was holding his breath until Cassandra answered on the third ring.

"Home Sweet Home, may I help you?"

Her voice was low and husky, just as he remembered it. He couldn't help but wonder how she'd sound when she woke in the morning—beside him. The intensity of his reaction surprised him. It hadn't been that long since he'd been with a woman, but this was different. Once the thought came to him, it was an impossible image to shake. He cleared his throat. "Do you have a room available for the night?"

He heard her quickly indrawn breath. "May I ask who is calling?"

"Dr. Andrade . . . Luke Andrade. I'm in town for Emma Turner's wake. I believe we met briefly."

She seemed to hesitate before saying, "Oh, yes. I remember. There are several large hotels not that far away. Let me see if I can find their numbers for you."

"So, you're booked up?"

"No," she admitted. "But I run a very small bed and breakfast. You'd probably be more comfortable in a hotel."

"I can sleep anywhere." Her reluctance to rent him a room was intriguing.

"I bet you can," she said in a droll tone, then gasped as if her words had surprised her. After a pause, she said, "I do have rooms available. Is it just for one night?"

He flushed at her question, like a schoolboy talking to a pretty girl for the first time. "Unless I find a reason to stay longer." He groaned. *Did I really just say that?*

"There isn't too much to do around here in the winter," she said quickly.

I have a few ideas. He shook his head. *Stop.*

"Are you hungry?" she asked.

You have no idea. His eagerness to see her again was un-nerving. He wasn't normally what most would call a spontaneous person. His surgical success relied on scientific discoveries. He based his decisions on experience and empirical evidence, not emotion and instincts. This defied logic, but, damn, it felt good.

Oblivious to where his mind had wandered, Cassandra said, "I was making fresh bread. It would go perfectly with beef stew if you'd like. I'll have it ready for when you arrive if you tell me when to expect you."

"Very soon. I believe you're only a couple blocks away."

He thought he heard her swear, but she continued on in a professional, friendly tone. "Great. I'll see you in a few minutes. Do you know the address?"

When he said he didn't, she quickly provided it and told him to park behind the building. Luke looked out his car's window for several moments after Cassandra hung up.

There are so many reasons why this is a bad idea.

But consequences be damned.

Consider me officially on vacation.

Chapter Two

*B*REATHE, CASSIE TOLD herself as she fluffed the bed pillows in the guest room farthest from her own. *He's a paying customer, no different than any other man who has stayed here before. So what if he's attractive? He's here for one night. Then he's gone.*

Feeling calmer, Cassie made her way back to the kitchen. The smell of fresh bread, still warm and wrapped in a towel on the table, blended with the mouthwatering fragrance from the stew heating on the stove. She closed her eyes and took a deep breath. During the years she'd lived with her mother and made do with empty cupboards and broken promises, she'd dreamed of places like this.

Home Sweet Home was more than a name she'd chosen for her bed and breakfast. It was a mantra, an ideal she still couldn't believe she'd achieved.

Not one part of the journey had been easy, but that made every moment even sweeter. Cassie opened her eyes and looked around at the new appliances and pristine counters. *I did this. I worked hard, paid for every bit of it myself, and now, if all goes well, I'll have someone to share it with.* She laid her hand gently on her flat stomach. *Nothing else matters.*

Cassie jumped at the knock on the side door. It swung open, and Luke Andrade stepped inside, his beautiful black hair coated with snow. He quickly closed the door behind him and shook himself off, then shot her a boyish smile that knocked the breath clean out of her.

"Sorry about the floor."

The floor? Cassie didn't care about her floor. What woman would when looking into those heavenly dark eyes? She and Luke stood there for a long moment, caught up in each other. He was undeniably the most gorgeous man she'd ever seen. Cassie considered herself moderately attractive, so he was way out of her league. Still, there was a warmth in his expression that made her feel as if he might be thinking exactly the same about her.

Cassie turned away, angry with herself for being tempted. She picked up a towel, walked over to him, and held it out, careful to keep her eyes averted from his. "Here. Dry off. You can hang your coat on the hook by the door."

He did. "It's quite a storm out there."

Cassie pointed at the table she'd set one place for. "Yes, looks like the weatherman was wrong. Shocker. Have a seat. Everything's ready."

He hesitated. "Did you already eat?"

Cassie filled a bowl with steaming broth and heaps of vegetables and meat. "No, but I'm fine." Her stomach growled, betraying her.

"Cassandra . . ."

Without turning away from the stove, Cassie corrected him. "Call me Cassie." Cassandra sounded stuffy and unapproachable. It didn't fit her. Nor did her mother's nickname for her: Cat. Jade Daiver loved to brag that her daughter had been born a survivor with an uncanny ability to land on her feet. It was a name Cassie had once tried to live up to. She'd become street-smart because she'd had to. She could take a punch because she'd been punched. But she chose to be softer . . . in her life and in her name.

"Cassie, join me." His voice was a caress of its own.

There was nothing suggestive or inappropriate about his request, but Cassie tensed. She wanted to say yes. The day had been an emotional one for her, and she didn't like how she felt around this man. Every inch of her was aware of his proximity. She didn't like feeling out of control. Cassie placed the bowl along with slices of warm bread on the table and turned away again. "I don't normally eat with my guests. Would you like coffee or something cool to drink?"

"Look at me." He'd said the words so softly Cassie thought she had imagined them at first. She raised her eyes to the triangle of his tie. "Are you okay having me here?"

No. Cassie kept her first response to herself. She forced a smile to her lips and said, "Of course. I run a bed and breakfast. Having guests is what I do." She turned away and busied herself by pouring a glass of water for him. She placed it beside his bowl of stew then retreated a short distance away. "Eat before everything gets cold."

He continued to stand beside the table. "I will . . . when you join me."

"I already told you I don't normally—"

"There is nothing normal about any of this, and I think you realize it too."

His velvet voice sent shivers through her. There was boldness in the way he looked at her, as if he had no doubt how the night would end. That made her angry but was also deliciously sexy. She frowned and met his eyes angrily. She needed to put an end to it.

Sleeping with a man like Dr. Luke Andrade had zero chance of leading anywhere good. He could be married. And even if he was single, he was only passing through. *I don't need a one-night stand.*

And I don't need the disappointment of watching how fast he'll run if I tell him I may be pregnant.

She met his eyes and said, "I'm pleased to provide a room for you tonight and feed you, but that's the extent of the services offered here."

"So, no sex after the stew?"

Cassie opened her mouth to say something cutting in response, but paused when she saw the twinkle of amusement in those luscious dark eyes. He was playful in a way she hadn't expected, and she didn't like how it made her like him more. "Exactly."

He let out a long, belabored sigh. "Well, we've cleared that up; now you can sit down and eat with me with full confidence that I have no expectations outside of conversation."

Folding her arms across her chest, Cassie held back stubbornly. Joining him was a dangerous first step toward giving in to the fantasy that anything between them was possible. "I'm serious."

Luke took his seat and picked up a spoon. "I admire your honesty. It can't be easy to take strangers into your home, especially men you don't know. I understand why you have rules about dining with guests, but today was a long day—for both of us. Sit down. I don't believe you want to eat alone tonight any more than I do."

His comment made Cassie feel foolish about how she'd openly proclaimed she wouldn't sleep with him. What if he hadn't even been thinking about her that way? *He's a doctor. He's gorgeous. He can probably have any woman he wants. No wonder he looks so amused. I am such an idiot.*

Without saying a word, Cassie filled a second bowl with stew and sat down across the table from him. She cut a slice of bread, buttered it without saying a word, and told herself to stop overreacting. Part of owning a bed and breakfast was being a good host. Normally it was a role she enjoyed. He'd flown in for a funeral. It was natural he wouldn't want to be alone. He might be really hurting. She frowned down at her food without taking a bite. "Did you know Emma very well?"

"Depends what you consider very well. I removed a tumor, but I wasn't her primary doctor. If she had been anyone else I may not have seen her again after the surgery, but we stayed in touch. I'll miss her."

Cassie pushed a potato around her bowl. "I wish I had met her. I moved here after she left, but I feel like I knew her. I've spoken to so many people about her. I'll miss her, too, even if that sounds crazy."

"It doesn't. The Turners told me their daughter had inspired your move here. Emma would have liked that."

They ate in silence for a few minutes. "So, you're a surgeon in New York City. That sounds exciting."

Luke gave her a small smile. "I used to think so."

There was something in his tone that resonated through Cassie. She met his eyes again and couldn't look away. She was right; he was hurting. What surprised her was it seemed to be about more than the passing of his friend. "Is your family in New York?"

A pained expression darkened Luke's face. "Yes."

Cassie understood that feeling well. "Family isn't easy."

"No, it's not." Luke sighed. "How about you? Are you close with yours?"

Emotion clogged Cassie's throat. She'd left behind her old life and everyone in it. "I don't have any family."

Luke rubbed a hand across his forehead. "You're probably lucky. I have three brothers who have spent most of their lives fighting. It's—"

"Exhausting." Cassie finished his sentence naturally. That's how loving her mother had been.

Luke smiled. "Yes. I've always smoothed over their arguments—encouraged them to forgive each other. But lately . . ."

Cassie laid her spoon down beside her bowl and leaned forward. "You started asking yourself who you would be without them. Who they would be without you. And if it's okay to be selfish enough to want to find out."

Luke's mouth opened and closed in surprise. Then he said, "Yes."

Without thinking, Cassie placed her hand on one of his. "It is. You deserve happiness just as much as they do." That simple touch sent a jolt through Cassie, and she pulled her hand back quickly and stood. "I'll get the key to your room."

"Don't—" Luke held out a hand to Cassie, but she retreated another step.

It was too easy to forget she didn't know Luke. Cassie turned away with determination and composed herself while she retrieved the key from a hook on the wall. What she was feeling had to be a side effect of attending a funeral earlier. Death, especially when it came to someone as young as Emma, had a way of shaking people up.

She handed Luke the key without making contact with his hand. "Your bedroom is upstairs at the end of the hall on the left. The stairs are right through that door. If you need anything there's an intercom in your room."

Please don't need anything.

Luke looked as if he wanted to say something, but instead he nodded. "Thank you, Cassie."

Warmth spread through her, and she knew he was thanking her for more than the room and the meal. "You're welcome. Good night."

"Good night."

Once Luke was out of the kitchen and Cassie heard the sound of his footsteps on the steps, she sank into a chair at the table. Safely alone, she raised both hands to her warm cheeks. If she were anyone but herself and they had met at another time, in another place, what she felt when she was near him might have led to something scandalously decadent.

She smiled shyly. *At least I'd like to think it would have.*

She pushed herself out of her seat and began to clear the dirty dishes. She heard the door to Luke's room open and close. *It's better this way.*

Her mood improved as she turned on the large ovens she'd purchased for Cassie's Creations. Life was full of unexpected revelations. Two years ago, if someone had told her she would be happy to spend hours in a kitchen baking, she'd have thought they were crazy. But she found joy and pride in making desserts people clamored for.

Cassie remembered when she'd first moved to Defiance and had stayed in this bed and breakfast. It had been love at first sight. Although the building was almost a hundred years old, it had been lovingly preserved. The décor was comfortably country. Fresh flowers, scented candles, soft colors, and even softer cushions. If a home were capable of it, Cassie would have said Home Sweet Home had embraced her.

The elderly couple who had owned it had been just as welcoming. They'd fed her what she'd considered the best meal of her life. Looking back, it had been rather simple fare, just a pot roast with the trimmings. Perhaps it'd had less to do with the food they'd served than with the warmth in their smiles and the genuine interest they'd taken in Cassie. Cassie had stayed with them for two weeks while seeking work in town.

Tilly had been friends with the couple who owned the

bed and breakfast and had been there the night they'd said they were considering selling the place and moving to the West Coast to live with their children.

Tilly had asked Cassie if she'd ever considered running a bed and breakfast. Cassie remembered explaining that, although she had some savings, she doubted it was enough to buy the place.

True to form, Tilly had said, "I didn't ask if you had the money to buy it, I asked if you had the desire to own it. If you want something badly enough, you make it happen. So, speak up, Cassie, do you want it?"

"Yes." Cassie remembered answering with everything in her.

Just as Tilly had said it would, everything fell into place once Cassie made owning the home her goal. She worked crazy hours waitressing at a restaurant in town. She saved for the down payment and took out a loan for the rest.

In the beginning money had been tight, but with Tilly's connections and a few brainstorming sessions, Cassie's Creations was born. Several restaurants and local shops featured her desserts on their menus, which provided income between guests. If she stayed the course and continued to work hard, she'd have her loan paid off in ten years.

As Cassie prepared the kitchen for a bout of baking, she flipped her recipe book open and ran a hand lovingly over a blank page. She'd intentionally left every other page blank. One day each of those pages would hold a photo of a child baking with her.

She briefly closed her eyes.

Good things happen when you stay focused. I'm where I want to be, making a living doing something I enjoy. She leaned back against the counter and wrapped both arms around her stomach. *Maybe it's wrong to want more than this, but I do.*

I want a baby, a family. I want to fill this home with love and laughter. And I don't want to wait, hoping some man will come into my life and make my dreams come true. I'll be thirty in a few years. What if he never comes? No, I'm not waiting on a whim of fate.

I'll make my own happy ending.

✧   ✧   ✧

LUKE PLACED HIS cell phone on the nightstand beside a twin-sized bed and laid his suit jacket across the back of a chair. He slowly removed his tie then tossed it on his jacket. Sitting on the edge of the bed he stepped out of his dress shoes and leaned forward onto his elbows.

When he closed his eyes he saw the beautiful face of the woman he could still hear downstairs in the kitchen. For some reason she brought back memories of a simpler time in his life.

He remembered how his brothers had responded to his first serious girlfriend. His oldest brother, Gio, had handed him a box of condoms and lectured him on the importance of using them. His youngest brother, Max, had chortled on the couch, a thoroughly amused audience. Nick had sauntered into the conversation, laid a hand on Luke's shoulder as if he were about to impart a pearl of wisdom and said,

"Luke, nice guys never get laid. And if they do, it's never that good."

Luke considered himself a nice man. *Maybe that's the problem.*

In his family, he was the one who didn't get angry. He'd seen the destructive nature of it too many times to allow himself that weakness. Instead, he'd always focused on what Uncle Victor had told him when he was a child. "Luke, you're an Andrade, and to an Andrade, family is everything."

Luke stood, stripped, then washed the day away beneath the hot spray of a shower. He didn't want to think about his family or anything he'd left behind in New York. He'd go back to them, but for a few days he wanted to wash it all away. What had Cassie said about family? "You start asking yourself who you would be without them. Who they would be without you."

Who am I?

Outside of the Turners, no one in the town knew much about him. In Defiance, Ohio, he wasn't a rich surgeon from a powerful family. He was just a man trapped in a storm, sleeping under the same roof as the most remarkable woman he'd ever encountered. A woman who had essentially already declared she wasn't interested in him.

Even if her eyes told a different story.

He hadn't seen a ring on her finger, but there was a chance she was already emotionally committed to a man. That particular thought hadn't occurred to him earlier. He dressed in lounge pants and a T-shirt then paced his bedroom restlessly.

Was she downstairs waiting for her lover to arrive?

He hadn't known her long enough to care what she did with her days or her nights.

But he did, a fact that frustrated him considering he was on sabbatical from caring.

The man he was in New York would have respected her hint to retire to his room for the night. However, he'd watched his brothers shamelessly pursue women they were interested in and succeed in winning them over.

That wasn't Luke's style. Women liked Luke, and that often led to sex. It wasn't something he'd spent much time thinking about.

He headed back down the stairs and stopped just before walking into the kitchen. His body tightened with anticipation at the sight of her. She was humming a soft tune, bent over in front of a large oven, checking the contents. The simple black dress she wore beneath her apron clung to her ass. When she straightened, her face was flushed, and she had an adorable smudge of frosting across one of her cheeks. In all his life he had never seen anything sexier. His senses were in pleasure overload. The heavenly scent of whatever sugary concoction she was baking only heightened the lust that rushed through him as he watched her. He wanted to taste every inch of her.

Luke fully understood the way the human body functioned. He'd even written a paper in college on the physical effects of desire and hormonal cascades. However, knowing which chemicals were responsible for the giddiness he felt didn't make it less real.

Being near her was so good it was painful. He shifted as his cock swelled enthusiastically in the loose confines of his lounge pants.

His movement must have caught her attention because she swung around with a spatula raised as if in defense. When she recognized him, she lowered it and said, "Sorry. Do you need something?"

He considered being honest, but chose a safe subject. "What are you baking?"

A smile spread across her face. "So, you're a sweets man. One guest told me she put on five pounds from the mere scent of my cupcakes. There were always a few missing when I woke in the morning, so I suspect she did more than smell them."

Luke would have said something witty, if anything had come to mind. Instead, he simply enjoyed how easily she was speaking to him and the wide smile on her face. She'd been guarded with him earlier, and he'd wondered if it was merely the challenge that made her so attractive. No, in that moment she was approachable and lighthearted and somehow even more beautiful. "Amazing."

"They really aren't. Cupcakes are an easy enough recipe, but I'll admit that I add a little something special to mine. I have a batch already cooling. Would you like one?"

"More than I should," Luke murmured.

Cassie's smile widened, and she piped frosting on a cupcake for him. "You're not alone. I don't know what it is about cupcakes. Maybe they remind people of every school party they had as a child, but no one can resist them." She removed the wrapping and held it out to him. "I never thought I'd spend so much of my time baking them, but they sell. Go ahead, indulge this once." Once? He doubted that indulging once in a woman like Cassie would ever be enough.

Unable to stop himself, Luke placed his hand on hers and brought the cupcake to his mouth. His eyes never left hers. He took a bite and felt her hand shake beneath his, but she didn't withdraw it at first. Rather, she traced his bottom lip with her pinkie then stepped back, leaving him holding the remainder of the cupcake and wondering if he'd lost his mind. *I can't resist her.* Just like the cupcakes he had indulged in as a schoolboy, he knew he couldn't leave Ohio without sampling her. "Cassie . . ."

She shook her head and held up a hand. "No. Forget it. I didn't mean to do that."

He took a step toward her. "Are you seeing anyone?"

Cassie frowned as he'd seen her do earlier. "It doesn't matter."

He placed the cupcake on the table and took another step closer. "It matters to me."

"Don't."

"Don't what."

"Don't look at me like that."

"Like you're the most beautiful woman I've ever seen? Like I want to taste that sweet mouth of yours as much as you thought I wanted the cupcake?" She didn't retreat, and he leaned close enough that his lips hovered above hers.

"Yes." Her breath was warm on his lips.

"One question: Are you?"

Her irises widened, a telltale sign she was equally as affected by him. "Am I what?" she whispered.

"Seeing someone."

"No."

Yes. He wanted to pull her to him and claim her mouth, but pleasure could also be in the anticipation. His breath turned ragged as he looked down into her eyes.

She put her hands up on his chest in a move that may have started as a push, but became more of a caress. Her voice was husky when she said, "Please don't." She closed her eyes, not yet removing her hands from his chest.

His hands went naturally to her hips. "You're just too tempting, Cupcake."

When her eyes opened again there was such a complex mixture of strength, yearning, and anger that he fought to catch his breath. Nothing he'd ever known had prepared him for Cassie.

She stepped back from him sadly. "I'm sorry. I know I'm sending you mixed signals, but you'll be heading back to New York as soon as the airport reopens. Some women would be into that, but I'm not." She turned away from him, paused momentarily, then bent to remove a pan of cupcakes from the oven.

"I don't have to."

She looked back at him. "Don't have to what?"

"Leave tomorrow. I'm technically on vacation."

She bit her bottom lip and glared at him. He couldn't understand the emotions raging in her brown eyes. "Check into a hotel tomorrow."

He couldn't walk away even when she turned her attention back to the stove. "Do you throw all of your guests out after one night, or just the ones you want to sleep with?"

When she spun to face him again, there was more passion in her eyes than anger. Still, her tone was harsh. "I'm . . . I don't—" She stopped mid-denial, then glared at him again. "I'm not having this conversation."

"Because I'm right."

"Because I'm not interested."

"I don't believe you." He closed the distance between them and laid his hands on the counter on either side of her. "I'm a doctor. We base our opinions on symptoms presented." He raised one hand to her throat. "Your pulse is racing. You're eyes are dilated. Your cheeks are flushed. You can lie to me and yourself, but your body knows what you want."

She licked her bottom lip nervously. "Is that supposed to be sexy?"

He grinned. "Yes."

The corner of her mouth twitched as if she almost smiled back at him. "I don't want to like you."

He kissed her lips quickly, nothing more than a tease of a touch. The sweetness of frosting from her lips lingered on his, insanely delicious, but he told himself not to rush. She looked conflicted about how she felt, and they'd only just met. When she came to him, he wanted it to be without reservation. Running his tongue over his top lip and armed with the knowledge that humor was the key to putting her at ease, he joked, "Too late, Cupcake."

She shook her head, but her cheeks were pink. "Good-night, Luke."

As he walked to the door of the kitchen, he felt her eyes on him and his skin burned for her touch. He glanced over his shoulder and winked at her. "I'll leave my door open in case you change your mind. Goodnight, Cassie. Thank you for sweetening my evening." His candid desire for her brought a smile to his face. He was a considerate lover, but Cassie brought out a playful side of him he'd never imagined he had. Before meeting Cassie, he'd imagined himself spending a week on a sandy beach. That idea had lost all appeal.

He wasn't leaving in the morning. He had no idea what that meant, but he'd never been more certain of anything. Back in his room, he removed his shirt and flopped on his back on the bed, folding his hands beneath his head.

He didn't bother to turn off the light. There was no way he'd sleep.

Chapter Three

"DAMN." CASSIE FINISHED decorating the final batch of cupcakes and looked around in frustration. She couldn't remember who she'd made them for. Normally she was very organized, however, the spreadsheet she always tacked to a corkboard near the fridge was missing. She remembered being distracted that morning. She'd been halfway out the door, heading to Emma's wake, when one of the coffee shops she baked for had called and added to their order.

It'd be helpful if I remembered which one. But the list is gone . . . along with my sanity.

She decided to pack them up and make awkward phone calls in the morning. She quickly glanced at the clock on the wall. *Shit. How could it already be two in the morning?*

What am I doing?

Besides hiding in my kitchen, she admitted wryly to herself. Yes, Luke was upstairs in a bedroom, just three doors down from hers, but that shouldn't matter. All of the doors had locks. Actually she enjoyed having people in her home. Usually her guests were married couples visiting their parents. Every once in a while she had a single traveler. One or two had attempted to flirt with her. However, Cassie always made it clear she wasn't interested and they usually respected that.

Luke shouldn't be any different. But he was. She brought her hand up to her lips and closed her eyes as she savored the memory of his touch. *He kissed me. Worse, I liked it.*

I should have told him not to call me Cupcake.

But I liked that, too.

Cassie cleaned the kitchen on autopilot as her mind raced. Luke might be attracted to her, but he didn't know her. When he said he could stay, he meant for a day or two. He was a successful doctor with a life outside of Defiance. He was looking for a casual hook-up and probably considered her the most available option.

But I'm not.

Easy or available.

Still, there was something disarmingly attractive about the way he smiled at her. It was as though they were already close, sharing some private joke. He had a way of talking to her that made her melt on the inside.

He was strong without needing to prove himself. She was used to men puffing up, strutting around like peacocks showing off, and often mentioning their financial prowess like it was an aphrodisiac instead of a turnoff. Luke had an easy confidence, almost a humble presence, that made Cassie think he must be a very successful surgeon.

She'd never connected with anyone the way she had with him. Every conversation they had felt . . . significant. That was the only word Cassie could think of to describe it.

Maybe everything feels more significant right after a funeral.

After the final batch of cupcakes was decorated and boxed, Cassie headed upstairs to her bedroom. She paused at the top, and her eyes flew to the open door of Luke's bedroom. She couldn't help it; she smiled. *He's a man of his word.*

Her mouth suddenly went dry as she imagined how the night would go if she took him up on his invitation. *Would it be so wrong?*

Yes, she told herself firmly and made her way to her own room. *One-night stands are like midnight fridge binges. You're hungry, it's there, and if you indulge you will regret it in the morning.*

Even if it's good. She closed the door of her bedroom and leaned back against it. *And it would be. I bet it would be fucking amazing.*

I need to stop swearing now that I might be a mother.

A mother.

Shit.

I could be pregnant. This is bad. He can't stay here another night.

Cassie pushed off from the door, stepped out of her shoes, and pulled her dress up over her head. She hung it on a hook beside the bathroom and shuffled inside. She dropped her bra into the hamper inside the bathroom. Her nightgown wasn't on the back of the door where she expected it to be. She shivered and looked around in frustration. *I need to get back to normal.*

Heading into the bedroom, she spotted her nightgown on a chair near her closet just as the lights flickered and went out. *No. No. No.*

Without giving her eyes time to adjust to the darkness, Cassie rushed across the room and tripped over an ottoman she'd forgotten was there. In just her panties, she fell to the floor with a loud thud. A string of profanity flew from her mouth as she checked if all her limbs were still intact before easing herself up onto her knees.

"Cassie? Are you okay?"

"Yes," she said in a rush, praying she'd locked her door.

"I heard a crash."

Cassie stood and tried to remember if there was anything else between where she was standing and her nightgown. "I'm fine." Unable to remember if she'd locked her door, Cassie scrambled for something to cover up with. "Go back to your room. I just need a minute." She followed the edge of her bed with her hand, knowing she was almost there when she felt the edge of the nightstand. She stubbed her toe on its leg, hunched over in pain, and knocked over a small glass lamp. The sound of it shattering on the wood floorboards echoed through the room. She couldn't see where the glass was, and she was barefoot. *Double shit.*

"Did something just break in there?" He sounded genuinely concerned.

"It sounds that way." She stepped onto the chair and steadied herself, trying to remember where she'd left her slippers.

Luke opened the bedroom door. "Where are you?"

"I'm in the corner of the room, but don't come over here. There's glass all over the floor."

"I have my shoes on."

"I'm not dressed."

"Oh," he said, his voice suddenly deeper than usual. "Not at all?"

"Not enough. So stay right where you are." Cassie felt around behind her for her nightgown. When her hand finally closed on it, she whipped it up over her head and slid it on. "Thank God."

"Why does that sound like you found clothes?"

The amused disappointment in his voice brought a reluctant smile to Cassie's lips. "Because I did. I'm serious about the glass, though. Do you have a flashlight?"

"Usually I use my cell phone, but since I bought one of the really smart ones, it's where it always is—charging."

"We can use the light on mine. If you walk straight into the room it's on the bureau."

"I could simply carry you over the glass."

"That's not a good idea."

"Because we both know where it would lead?" When Cassie didn't say anything, Luke continued, "We may have just met, but I know you feel it, too. Whatever this is. Why deny it? We're both adults. We're alone. There's nothing wrong with cutting loose for a change. Aren't you tired of always doing the right thing?"

His voice was deep and seductive. A battle raged within Cassie. She wanted to tell him to get out. She wanted to invite him to stay. She whispered, "No."

"Ever wonder who you'd be if you didn't always do the right thing?"

If another man had asked that, Cassie would have thought it was a line. Instead, there was something touching about the way he asked the question. Luke seemed like a man at a crossroads in his life. Cassie told herself whatever he was going through was none of her business. She'd barely figured herself out. She didn't have the answers he needed. Still, it was impossible not to wonder what had brought him to a place where he would ask such a question. She answered him honestly. "Unfortunately, I know exactly who I would be, and I'm not that person anymore."

A beam of light shone in her direction as he turned on her phone. He studied her face for a long moment. The earlier playfulness was gone. "I won't pretend I don't want you."

Perched high on the chair in the corner of her room, Cassie tried not to look as ridiculous as she felt. "We all want things we can't have, Luke. You're on vacation. You made a pass at me. I turned you down. You find that exciting. But it doesn't change that you'll be back in New York before you know it, and if I say yes, I'll be some woman you slept with on your trip to Ohio. I don't want that."

"I could—"

"You said that before. Stay for what—another day? A

week? Then what? You don't get to come into my life and mess it up; do you hear me?"

In the darkness behind the stream of light, his face was hidden from her view. "I would never—"

Wrapping her arms around her waist, Cassie said, "Don't say it. I've heard it too many times. I can't risk it again. Not now. Not when I'm finally happy."

Luke walked over to Cassie and handed her the cell phone. He stood in front of the chair with a torn expression on his face. "Someone hurt you, Cassie, but it wasn't me."

She met his eyes cautiously.

He held out his hand to her. "I will carry you across the glass, and you will let me."

She didn't move. "How do I know . . . ?" Her voice trailed away, leaving an unspoken question hanging between them. *How do I know I can trust you?*

"You know."

She put a hand on his shoulder, and he lifted her into his arms, carrying her to the door of her room. As he walked, the glass crunched beneath his shoes. At the door, he stepped out of his shoes and lowered her to the floor. The light on her phone went off, and they were standing in the dark once again. Within the intimate circle of his arms, she felt his arousal against her stomach and shivered. Conflicting emotions swirled within her. He'd said he wanted her and was sporting impressive evidence that he did. She knew she should be worried, but she felt oddly safe within the circle of his strong arms.

She hoped her excitement wasn't as obvious as his. She knew she should pull away, but she was getting wet even as she mentally recounted the many reasons she couldn't sleep with him that night.

"Do you have flashlights?" he asked, his voice sounding a little strangled.

She coughed nervously at the double meaning. "No."

"Candles? How about a generator?"

"I have candles downstairs. I meant to buy a generator, but . . ."

"Without power, will the heat work?"

"No." It wasn't something that felt like an impending problem, given her skin was on fire everywhere it contacted Luke's muscular body. She told herself it was time to turn her phone light back on, but there was something unreal, almost dreamlike, about standing in the dark together. "But we can make a fire."

He tensed against her, groaned, then took one of her hands in his. "Let's go find those candles and build a fire before I change my mind and take you right here on the stairs."

And I'd let you, Cassie thought. She turned her phone light on and illuminated the stairs, careful not to look up at Luke. "There are blankets and pillows downstairs. We can pull two couches close to the fire. It'll be fine."

Even in the dark, Cassie felt his eyes on her face. "Cassie, I heard what you said earlier. Nothing will happen between us . . . tonight."

There was so much Cassie wanted to say. She wanted to explain to him if they had met years before she might have spent the night in his arms. God knows, if she'd met him in her early twenties she wouldn't have thought twice about being with him. But she'd chosen a different path, and in her mind, a better one.

She caught herself before she placed a hand on her stomach. It was a path she might not be on alone anymore. Which was more than enough reason to say no to Luke.

She opened her mouth, about to regurgitate some of her story to him, but when she met his eyes the words fell away. He was looking down at her with a protective, possessive expression that shook her. What would it be like to belong to a man like that? Even if it were only for a night.

I'll never know.

Cassie squeezed his hand. "Thank you."

He continued to look down at her, then the boyish smile that had melted her defenses earlier returned, and he said, "Come on, Cupcake, let's go build that fire."

He led the way down the main stairs, and despite everything Cassie told herself, she knew she would probably have followed him right back to his room if that had been his choice. She couldn't say yes to him, but she was equally unable to say no.

A SHORT WHILE later, Luke lay back on a couch in Cassie's living room and tucked the blankets around himself in frustration. He looked across at Cassie who was bending over in front of the fire, placing another log onto it. He would have offered to do it himself, but each time she stood in front of it, the firelight made her nightgown transparent, and as he was discovering, he was only human.

He doubted a single one of his brothers would have spent the night on one couch if the woman they desired was on the other. *I told her nothing would happen tonight.*

Why?

Because I'm a nice guy.

And nice guys don't get . . .

Returning to the other couch he had pushed beside his, Cassie crawled beneath the covers. He'd placed the furniture so he and Cassie were at an angle, not only to be warmed by the fire, but also to see each other. She tucked a hand beneath her head, watching him as the sexual tension between them became almost unbearable. "Tell me about your life in New York."

Her request took Luke by surprise. He'd been asked the question a hundred times, but usually it was part of a tedious conversation. *What is it like to be from such a wealthy family? Do you really work? Why?* "What would you like to know?"

"I know it's none of my business, but . . ."

Luke propped himself up onto one elbow. No matter what she asked, he wanted to answer. She wanted to know him better. He certainly wanted to know her. All of her. Intimately. Repeatedly. Then once again until they were both too exhausted to continue. "Ask me anything."

She searched his face before answering. "I'm curious

about your brothers. You said they don't get along. If they're anything like you, I can't imagine that."

Her interest seemed sincere, and it occurred to him she probably had no idea he came from an immensely wealthy family. There was no reason for her to know. His family was well-known in New York, but he doubted many out in Ohio knew of them. It was refreshing to simply be looked upon as a man and not a doctor who chose his own schedule because he'd donated a wing to the hospital. "My oldest brother, Gio, has been the head of the family ever since my father died. Honestly, probably before then. Some people think he's stern, but he sees himself as our protector. He always has. My next brother, Nick, is the exact opposite. Or, at least, he was for a very long time. He's coming around. You'd like him. He could charm candy from a baby. And he's hilarious. My youngest brother, Max, is a true independent soul. Tracking him down is practically a family pastime."

"They don't sound so awful."

Luke frowned. "Did I say they were?"

"You said they were exhausting."

Nodding, Luke said, "I did, didn't I? They can be. Gather them together for more than five minutes, and sometimes I feel like a lion trainer trying to keep the peace."

Cassie tucked a curl behind her ear. "How do you think they'd describe you?"

Luke didn't want to answer that. He knew. They'd told him often enough. Finally, he said, "Unrealistically optimistic. It's not a label most surgeons wear proudly."

"I'd guess not. But it's probably a good trait for a brother to have."

As lost as he felt, Cassie's version of him was more than a little appealing. She had a way of taking what he least liked about himself and making it sound normal, if not admirable. Luke fluffed his pillow then flopped down onto it, looking up at the ceiling. "I'm coming to the conclusion it's not a good trait in any situation." He turned his head so he could see Cassie. "What about you? You said you don't have family. Was there an accident?"

Cassie pulled the blanket tighter around herself. She closed her eyes. "No. Sorry, Luke. Can we talk in the morning? I'm tired."

So, she didn't want to discuss her family. It made him even more curious. He knew next to nothing about her except she'd moved from Detroit a couple years ago and started a new life in Defiance. Even though her eyes were firmly shut, he knew she was still awake. "There is nothing you could say that would shock me, Cassie. Or make me like you less."

Cassie punched her pillow and rolled away from him. "Said like a man who has never spent a day in hell. Goodnight."

Luke wanted to apologize. He wanted to ask her a hundred questions, but he covered his eyes with his arm and told himself to go to sleep.

Hell came in many forms. Emotional. Physical. Combinations of both.

He had no right to ask her to describe hers if he was unwilling to share his.

Not yet.

Chapter Four

C ASSIE WOKE TO the morning sunlight; the room was warm even though the fire had gone out. Power must have returned sometime during the night. She walked to the window and pushed back the blue curtains. A path to her front door had been cleared. She walked through her small kitchen. From the window, she saw the back path had also been cleared.

Luke's coat was hanging by the door, and there were gloves on the kitchen table he must have worn while he shoveled. He was back inside, but where was he?

Cassie put a pot of coffee on, then called the restaurants that had open orders for the cupcakes. Two were closed because of the weather. One was open.

"We have everyone busy shoveling us out. Could you drop them off to us?" asked Bonnie Duvall, the owner of one of the busiest coffee shops in town. Bonnie and her husband, Greg, had been the first in town to put in an order from Cassie's Creations. There wasn't much Cassie wouldn't do for them.

"Absolutely. How soon do you need them?" The storm

had ended. Her street looked passable, if not yet clear.

"Before eleven?"

"See you then," Cassie said. She checked the time on her phone. She had just enough time to shower, pack up her SUV, and make the delivery. She went to the closet to grab a dustpan and broom, but it was missing. *Figures. Everything got confused yesterday, but I'll put it all back in order today.*

Cassie stepped into her snow boots and decided they were also anti-glass boots until she located the dustpan. She headed up to the second floor of the house. Luke's door was open, and Cassie thought she heard the sound of his voice inside, but she didn't let herself stop. She raced into her room, closed the door behind her, and locked it. *No surprises today. No mooning at him. Yesterday was the result of an extremely emotional day for both of us. I'm sure he's just as relieved as I am that nothing happened last night.*

Cassie looked around her bedroom and realized the glass from the night before had been cleaned up. The broom and dustpan were leaning against the wall near a small wastebasket. Cassie's eyes misted. She wasn't used to being taken care of. Tilly offered her help now and then, but that was different. She was a friend. Luke was . . . nothing.

And leaving.

So what if he picked up a little glass?

Shoveled for me?

Men will do anything to get into a woman's bed. They turn on the charm until they get what they want. Then, wham, they're gone.

She gave herself a stern look in her bathroom mirror.

Your days of being naïve are over. Let it go. Let him go. Don't do this to yourself.

She took a short, hot shower, blew her hair dry, and threw on jeans and a blouse. She considered putting on makeup but stopped herself. *It's better if he doesn't find me attractive. He needs to leave. Today.*

Squaring her shoulders, she walked out of her bedroom with the intention of telling him she'd prepare a quick breakfast for him, but he'd have to eat alone because she had a delivery to make. She'd write up his bill, give him directions to the airport or a local hotel. And that would be the end of it.

Her resolve wavered when she saw him in the hallway. He was dressed in jeans as well, with a dark blue T-shirt that clung to his muscular chest in the sexiest way. His easy smile almost sent her scurrying back to her room. "Morning, Cupcake."

Unable to take her eyes off him, Cassie waved toward the stairs absently. "I have a delivery to make."

"I'll go with you," he said and strode over to where she was.

Cassie swallowed hard. "You stay and eat breakfast. I have to go." She couldn't focus when he was so close. He smelled of soap and a light aftershave that made her want to lean in closer.

He slid a hand beneath the hair on the nape of her neck and pulled her forward a step. Without a word, he gently claimed her lips. Cassie was too shocked to respond at first. She put a hand up between them, then gave herself over to the pleasure of his mouth on hers. Of the beat of his heart against her hand. He broke off the kiss before it deepened and brought his hands to her waist as if to pull her fully against him. "That and a coffee is all I need . . . for now."

"Cassie," Tilly's voice rang through the house. "Are you here? I saw your car outside."

Neither Cassie nor Luke moved at first, frozen like two guilty children. Cassie whispered, "That's my neighbor, Tilly. She has a key."

Luke gave her a sexy smile that brought a flush to her cheeks. "Good to know."

Cassie called to Tilly, "I'm upstairs. I'll be down in a minute."

"Just checking in to see how you made out in the storm. We lost power. I figured you did, too. Did you get your baking done?" Despite Tilly's age, she was fast on her feet. She was halfway up the stairs when she saw Luke and stopped dead. "Well, look at you two."

Cassie jumped back from Luke. "Tilly, this is Dr. Andrade. He's in town for Emma's funeral."

Tilly looked back and forth between them. "Dr. Andrade. I've heard good things about you."

Luke went halfway down the stairs to meet her and offered his arm to Tilly. "Please, call me Luke."

Tilly took his arm and began to descend the stairs with him. "He's a doctor, Cassie."

"I know," Cassie said with a grimace. Tilly wasn't known for keeping many thoughts to herself, but Cassie couldn't see a way to break the two apart.

Tilly gave Luke's arm a pat. "And so strong. Are you the one who shoveled Cassie out?"

Luke winked at Cassie as the three of them entered the kitchen. "I couldn't sleep anyway."

Tilly caught Cassie's blush and a wide smile spread across her face. "It's so nice to have a man around here again."

"Again?" Luke asked. Although his tone was casual, the look he gave Cassie was that of a territorial male assessing if he had competition.

Cassie poured Luke a cup of coffee and handed it to him abruptly. "It's a shame you have to get back to New York this morning, Dr. Andrade. Let me get you that bill you asked for."

Tilly made herself a cup of coffee. "You're leaving so soon, Luke?"

"Apparently," Luke said dryly, taking a sip of the piping hot brew.

Cassie bent over the small built-in desk in the kitchen and wrote out a bill for one night. "I'm giving you a discount since a full breakfast is usually included in the price of the room."

Tilly made a disapproving sound. "What? You're not even feeding him?" Tilly sat down at the kitchen table. "He's easy on the eyes. Sweet as your pecan pie. And he has a job. Men like that don't come through this town every day. If I were your age, I'd show you what to do with a man like that. And it's not starve him half to death."

Cassie rolled her eyes toward the ceiling in mortification. Luke looked pleased with himself. He sat next to Tilly and said something to her that made her blush and swat him. "Cassie, you're a fool if you run this one off."

"I'm not running him off," Cassie said impatiently and put a completed bill on the table beside Luke. "He has patients waiting for him. Don't you, Dr. Andrade?"

Luke sat back in his chair with a sexy cockiness. "Usually the answer would be yes, Cupcake, but I'm technically on vacation this week. So, I'm not in much of a hurry to go anywhere."

Tilly's smile grew as she watched their exchange.

Cassie glared at him, but Luke smiled back at her shamelessly. She grabbed her coat off its hook and snapped, "I have a delivery to make. Tilly, do you want me to drop you off on my way?"

Tilly stirred creamer into her coffee. "I don't mind keeping Luke company while you're gone. He and I can just sit here and get to know each other until you get back."

Cassie froze midway through buttoning her coat. "Dr. Andrade, can I speak to you for a minute?"

Luke didn't budge. "Luke."

"Luke," Cassie said between gritted teeth, "could you help me carry a few things to the car?"

Tilly slapped the table gleefully as Luke stood up. "That's a great idea. Take him with you. Feed him while you're out as a thank you for helping you shovel. Don't worry about me. I'll putter around here until you two return."

In a forced pleasant tone, Cassie said, "You know who I saw outside a few minutes ago? Myron. He might still be out there. Should I tell him you were looking for him?"

Cassie shared a long look with Tilly, a standoff of sorts. Tilly blinked first. "Oh, fine. I can see why you'd want your privacy. I don't need a ride, though. My son can pick me up. If he complains, I'll remind him why he's my chauffeur now."

Luke told Tilly it had been nice to meet her. He shrugged on his coat and didn't seem to mind at all that Cassie piled box upon box of cupcakes into his arms. Did he have to be so damn nice?

She grumbled to herself as she walked out of the house until she caught him watching her with interest. She opened the hatch and secured the boxes in the back of her SUV without looking at him again. "You don't have to come with me."

He stepped closer and waited until she raised her eyes to his. When she did, he said, "I want to."

She searched his face for a sign of what he was thinking. "You know you can't stay here tonight."

He caressed one of her cheeks gently. "Because you don't trust me? Or yourself?" He brushed his thumb lightly across her bottom lip then brought his other hand up so he was cupping her face. "Is it because you know this will happen?"

By the time his lips closed over hers, Cassie had gone onto her tiptoes to meet him halfway. It didn't matter that she knew it was a bad idea. Unlike the brief, almost chaste kisses they'd shared earlier, this one was explosively passionate. Cassie gripped the front of his coat desperately, clinging to him as desire shook through her body. She opened her mouth to him, inviting him to deepen the kiss and moaned with pleasure when he did.

His tongue flicked across her lips, then plunged to meet hers, circling it in a primitive, sensual dance. The cold was forgotten along with any care about someone watching. His hand moved to the nape of her neck, tightening possessively. Cassie writhed against him, reveling in how he seemed as blown away by the kiss as she was.

When he broke off the kiss, he laid his forehead on hers and closed his eyes as if gathering strength. Their ragged breaths were visible in the cold air. Cassie struggled to reconcile her scrambled thoughts.

She didn't want this.

But, oh, how she wanted this.

He raised his head, and she couldn't look away from his truly spectacular brown eyes. At first she'd thought they were almost black, but in the bright light of day, she saw warm flecks of amber. He was a man who became more beautiful each time she looked at him.

"You don't know what you do to me, Cassie. I want to take you, right here, right now, in the middle of all those damn boxes. You make me feel alive in a way I didn't know I was missing. How do I walk away from this?"

Cassie tried to catch her breath. She believed him because he'd articulated exactly how he made her feel. She wanted to deny it, but she couldn't while looking into his eyes. "What's the alternative? I don't want to be your vacation fling."

"It would never be like that," he denied hotly.

She gently removed the hand he had on her face, but

continued to hold it. "That's exactly what it would be. It's all it could be. My life is here. And you have a job and family waiting for you in New York. There is nowhere this could go." *This is where I tell him I might be pregnant. Right now.* Cassie let herself soak in how good it felt to be desired by Luke. She knew everything would change in a moment. "And there's something I need to tell you . . ."

"If it's about the man Tilly mentioned, I don't care about him. He's not here now. Give me tonight, and I'll make love to you until you can't remember anyone before me."

Cassie cocked her head to one side. She hadn't been with anyone since she'd moved to Defiance. Tilly had probably been referring to the previous owner of the bed and breakfast. "Simon was—"

Luke pulled her to him and growled, "I told you, he doesn't matter."

He's jealous. Luke had that primal, possessive look on his face again that sent Cassie's heart into a wild beat as her body quivered with need. He held her to him, and she couldn't resist. She needed to feel him. She slid a hand down between them and boldly caressed the bulge of his engorged cock through his jeans. He sucked in an audible breath.

Luke leaned down and whispered into her ear, "Oh, Cupcake, you're torturing me, but don't stop."

Lost in a daze of desire, Cassie struggled to regain control of herself even as she continued to stroke him. He was so hard, so big. Her panties were soaked at the idea of how he would feel inside her. "We shouldn't do this."

He kissed her neck hotly. "Or this."

Cassie arched her neck to the side. He kissed his way down it, then pulled the top of her coat open and rained kisses across her collarbone. Breathlessly, Cassie said, "I don't know how to say no to you."

He raised his head, his breathing as ragged as her own. "Then say yes."

A man's voice startled both of them. "Is my mother inside?"

Cassie jumped back from Luke. Tilly's son, Jimmy, was in his early fifties. He'd moved in with his mother after a divorce and never moved out. He was normally vaguely pleasant, but at that moment he had a disapproving look on his face. Cassie fought back a nervous, guilty giggle.

"She's probably still in the kitchen."

"I can see why she called me."

Luke stood straighter and looked about to say something, but Cassie caught his eye and silently pleaded for him not to. Luke kept his comment to himself, but didn't look happy about it. Cassie decided introductions could wait for another day. She closed the hatch of her SUV. "Well, we're off to make a delivery."

Jimmy didn't look convinced. He walked to the house without saying another word.

Suddenly feeling the cold, Cassie bolted for the warmth of her car. She settled into the driver's seat while Luke quite happily took the passenger seat. With both hands on the steering wheel, Cassie said dryly, "I bet he doesn't let Tilly come over again until you're gone."

Luke ran a warm hand up and down one of her thighs. His caress held a promise of more. "That's probably for the best, Cupcake."

Cassie knew Luke was right, but thought it safer not to agree. She started the car and pulled out onto the road, trying to ignore how her body was throbbing with need for his touch. She wasn't an inexperienced virgin. She'd slept with a few men. Some had been better than others. None had made her feel the way Luke did.

Just a look from him, a heated glance, and Cassie was squirming in her seat. How could she walk away from something like that?

He'd asked her that question, and she honestly didn't know the answer.

She was beginning to fear that maybe she couldn't.

LUKE CONSIDERED HIMSELF a levelheaded man. He didn't rush into decisions. He gathered information, came to logical conclusions, and acted upon them. He admitted his family had the ability to derail him sometimes, but he'd never met a woman before who made him feel off balance—excitedly so.

If it was simple female companionship he was seeking, that was plentiful back in New York. He couldn't imagine he'd be alone long if he flew off to that beach he'd considered traveling to. Neither option held appeal anymore.

What had Cassie said? She didn't want to be just a woman he'd slept with on his vacation. He'd denied it would be like that, but her concerns were valid. Although he was enjoying stepping out of his life, he had no intention of staying in Defiance. Eventually he'd have to go back.

Not wanting to think about that yet, he turned his attention back to Cassie and her beautiful profile. She was concentrating on navigating the snow-covered streets. The care she took while approaching each stop sign was endearing.

The feel of her hand on his cock was still vivid enough to keep him uncomfortably hard. He wanted to tell her to pull over so he could taste her sweet lips again. They were as irresistible as the frosting on her sugared cupcakes. If their exchanges so far were anything to go by, sex with her was going to be phenomenally tasty.

"How did you start a baking business?" he asked. It wasn't the most thought-provoking question, but he hoped it would distract him temporarily from how much he wanted her. He literally ached for her.

She glanced at him quickly then kept her eyes glued to the road. "It started with the cupcakes. I enjoyed baking them for my guests. I'd send them away with boxes of them. Some guests went to town and told people about them. Tilly made some calls and before I knew it, Bonnie and Greg were ordering cases of them for their restaurant. Now I sell to quite a few places."

"What did you do before you moved here?" Luke asked.

Her lips pressed together unhappily. "I worked in a sandwich shop in downtown Detroit."

He knew he had touched upon a topic she wasn't comfortable with by the way her expression tightened. "I imagine living in Defiance is quite different."

"It is," Cassie said abruptly. "I'm happy here. Happier than I can ever remember being."

He gave her thigh a supportive squeeze. "And you're afraid being with me could change that?"

She glanced at him again quickly. "I don't want to get all heavy, and someone like you could never understand."

"Like me?" He frowned.

She took a corner with extra care. "You're good-looking, obviously successful at what you do. Bet you went to a private school."

"And you are a gorgeous, independent woman who runs both a bed and breakfast and a side business. We're not as different as you think."

"No? Have you ever been so hungry you stole food by hiding it in your coat? Did you ever sleep beneath trash bags in a park because your mother was binging on drugs with a boyfriend, and anywhere was safer than your home?"

"No," he said slowly, absorbing what she'd said. She didn't come across as a woman who had been through the life she alluded to. Imagining her in either situation she'd just described filled him with anger and sadness, along with a desire to protect her even though the threat she described was in the past.

"You said you had no family. What happened to your mother?"

Cassie shook her head once. "I don't know, and I don't care. I haven't spoken to her since I left Detroit. I lived with her until I was eighteen. Then I got my own place, but she followed me. She said she needed me. All she did was steal money from me, bring strange men into my apartment, and apologize. I'm so sick of people who think they can do whatever they want as long as they regret it afterward. Being sorry isn't enough. Not if you go right back and do it again."

Even though her tone was calm, she seemed tense. He needed to hear the rest of her story. "You said Emma inspired your move to Defiance."

Cassie shrugged. "I was feeling trapped in my life in Detroit. Then I heard Emma's story. She sounded so brave. I wanted to be like her. And the way she described this town . . . I didn't think places like it existed. I was ready to defy my mother and everything she represented, and I thought a place named Defiance might be the answer. Even when I came here—I think I did it half expecting to be disappointed. But I wasn't. The original owners of Home Sweet Home welcomed me like family returning home to them. My neighbors watch out for me because they know I live alone. That's why I went to Emma's funeral. I wanted to thank her for bringing me here."

With each word, and each picture she painted of her journey, he found it more difficult to breathe. More than anything else he wanted to pull her into his arms and hold her. "Cassie . . ."

Something in his tone made her frown. "I don't want your pity. I'm telling you this to show you why we don't make sense."

He gave her thigh another squeeze. He couldn't deny they had had very different childhoods. He'd never known a day of hunger. He'd never been cold. But if she thought he pitied her, she was wrong. "All you've proven is you're even more amazing than I first thought."

Cassie blinked back tears as she pulled into a parking spot in front of a coffee shop. "I'm not. I'm really a hundred times more messed up than you think. I haven't even told you—"

With his hand around her chin she was forced to look at him. "Stop, Cassie. Stop trying to push me away before we have a chance to get to know each other."

Her eyes burned with an emotion he couldn't determine. "What do you want from me, Luke?"

He gave her a light kiss because he didn't know how else to answer her. He didn't know how to answer himself.

She kissed him back with a hunger that he was careful not to take advantage of.

She was afraid he would mess up her new life?

Didn't she know she was turning his upside down?

Chapter Five

"TELL ME EVERYTHING. What is Dr. Andrade like?" Bonnie pulled Cassie aside as Luke helped Bonnie's husband, Greg, carry the boxes of cupcakes to the kitchen of the small restaurant. There were only about thirty tables in the whole place, but they were always full. Fresh cut flowers on every table, beautiful linens, and the best food in fifty miles made it worth the drive—even in a snowstorm. It also happened to be the place to hang out to know what was going on in the town.

"Excuse me," an older woman asked from a nearby table. "May I have more coffee, please?"

Bonnie held up one finger at the customer. "In a minute, Dot. Dr. Andrade is staying at Cassie's place. I need to get the scoop."

"Is that who just walked through with your husband? Oh, he's good-looking. Will he be here long? My daughter works right around the corner. I can have her here in five minutes."

Two younger women from the next table chimed in. "That was Dr. Andrade? He is hot. Is he really single?"

Bonnie flipped her long blonde braid over her shoulder and waved an impatient hand at them. "No one is bringing anyone in here to meet him. He's already taken." She pulled Cassie through the "Employees Only" doorway. Once they were alone, Bonnie gripped Cassie's hand with excitement. "Do you know how many women are going to be disappointed when they find out Dr. Andrade is off the market."

Cassie gently removed her hand from Bonnie's. "What are you talking about?"

"Come on, it's me. Bonnie. I'm not going to judge you. I think it's wonderful to finally see you with a man."

Cassie's eyes widened, and she referenced the door behind her with thumb. "You mean, Dr. Andrade? He's just here to help me drop off your order. Maybe have breakfast. Then he's heading back to New York."

Bonnie folded her arms over her chest and shot Cassie a skeptical look. "Really? So the two of you were snowed in last night, all alone, and nothing happened? That's the story you're sticking to?"

Cassie raised her chin with determination. "No. I mean, yes. Nothing happened."

With a tap of her foot, Bonnie countered, "Edward from the hardware store came in about five minutes ago to pick up his lunch order. He said Jimmy told him you were kissing Dr. Andrade in your driveway."

A hot blush spread up Cassie's neck and warmed her cheeks. She didn't like getting caught in a lie, and she was still adjusting to small-town life. "It might have looked that way, but Luke was actually helping me carry boxes to my car."

Bonnie chuckled. "You're such a bad liar. And I don't understand why you're so embarrassed. Hell, if I had hooked up with someone like him, I'd be bragging about it."

That brought a reluctant smile to Cassie's face. "You're married."

Bonnie squeezed Cassie's shoulder. "Yes. Which is exactly why I have to live vicariously through you. Come on, spill."

Cassie was used to bottling up her feelings. Things were safer when kept secret. Money was better hidden. It wasn't like that in Defiance. When she had first moved, she'd been uncomfortable when she'd discovered she was a frequent topic of discussion. However, time had shown her it wasn't malicious. Her first summer, before she'd been able to afford her own lawnmower, a couple of her neighbors had taken turns helping her out. She, in turn, took them homemade chicken soup when they were sick. The gossip chain became something Cassie was grateful for once she realized it was how the town stayed connected. Of course, she'd never had something like this spreading around. What she felt for Luke was scary enough without trying to defend or explain it. "We kissed. That's it. But he really is leaving."

Bonnie's face split in a huge smile. "Just tell me, was it as wonderful as we're all fantasizing it would be?"

Cassie smiled right back and admitted, "Better."

Bonnie fanned her face with one hand. "I knew it." She looked Cassie over with a critical eye and tucked a loose hair into Cassie's ponytail. She reached into the pocket of her apron and pulled out lipstick, then turned Cassie in the direction of a mirror on the wall. "If you want a shot at keeping a man like that, you have to put in a little effort."

"He's not staying," Cassie repeated, but she applied a light coat of the pink lipstick.

Bonnie handed her mascara and eyeliner. "Yet."

Cassie applied both. "Won't it seem strange that I came in here without makeup, and I'm walking out there with it on?'

Bonnie nodded and unbuttoned the two top buttons of Cassie's blouse. "No, now he won't notice. Well, he'll notice, but he won't put much thought into it."

Cassie protested, "It's not that simple."

"Yes, it is. You keep saying you want to settle down and have a family here. How are you going to do that without a man?"

Cassie's hand went automatically, protectively, to her stomach. She'd been very careful to go out of town for treatments. No one knew her secret. "It'll happen one way or another. But hooking up with a man who is just passing through is not part of my plan."

Pursing her lips, Bonnie said, "Cassie, I adore you, but you have to stop hiding in your bed and breakfast." Cassie opened her mouth to say something, but Bonnie started speaking again before she was able to get a word out. "Look at us. I took a chance on you, and we've become friends. You don't know what's possible until you try. And if you're afraid of getting your heart broken? Darling, that could happen to any of us at any time. Aunt Bea's husband left her after forty years. He's not going to find better than her, so he'll be back. But she's not sitting at home moping about it. There is no shame in taking a risk on love." She paused. "Unless you sleep with half the men in town, then it's a little much for most people to handle."

Feeling overwhelmed, Cassie rubbed one of her temples with her index finger. "There's not much chance of that happening."

"Exactly. So don't worry. Even if you get pregnant, I bet that man makes beautiful babies."

Babies?

Cassie closed her eyes and grimaced. As the only man I've been seen with in public, if I am pregnant, people are going to assume it's his. *Oh, my God.*

Bonnie hugged her. "I was joking. Use a condom and have some fun. Girl, loosen up. No matter what happens, you'll have an amazing story to tell."

"Tell?"

Bonnie smiled cajolingly. "To at least me, and maybe Tilly."

"Tilly?" Cassie's voice went up several octaves.

"She was a wild one when she was young. Her parents tried to send her to an all-girls' school to calm her down, but she gave them a run for their money. Don't let her fool you. She has some good stories about dating before she was married. Ask her sometime."

Cassie was grateful to hear Luke and Greg approaching. Bonnie's attitude reflected what Cassie loved most about Defiance. The town definitely had boundary issues when it came to getting involved in each other's lives, and Cassie found that both heartwarming and terrifying.

Very similar to how she felt each time she spoke to Luke.

Some risks did pay off. She'd risked everything on this town, and it had changed her life for the better. She walked out of the storage room with Bonnie and met Luke's eyes. The warmth of his smile and the way he didn't disguise how happy he was to see her took her breath away. The slight pink that warmed his cheeks when his eyes fell to her cleavage made her almost giddy with pleasure.

I won't know what's possible if I don't give this a try.

And I'll spend the rest of my life asking myself what might have happened.

ESPECIALLY AFTER HEARING about Cassie's childhood, Luke enjoyed watching her with her friends. It was obvious Cassie and the restaurant owner were close. And if the grilling he'd received from the husband was anything to go by, her friends were more than a little protective of her. He'd half expected Greg to come right out and demand to know what his intentions were. Which wouldn't have gone well since Luke didn't know yet himself. All he knew for sure was the ten or so minutes they had spent apart had felt like an eternity.

Bonnie shook Luke's hand then looked to her husband as if asking his opinion. Greg shrugged and nodded in what appeared to be a non-verbal endorsement of Luke. Bonnie continued to shake Luke's hand, but now with more enthusiasm. "You two are staying for breakfast, right?"

"If Dr. Andrade—" Cassie started to say, but Luke cut her off.

"We'd love to." Luke placed a possessive hand on Cassie's lower back. He wasn't used to feeling possessive about a woman, not even one he'd dated for a prolonged time. He'd considered himself above jealousy, but he sent a warning look to a man he'd caught watching Cassie when they'd walked in.

Bonnie led them to a booth and gave them menus before heading to the kitchen with her husband. He and Cassie looked over the menus long enough that it became awkward. Without looking up from his, Luke said, "I'll book a room in a hotel."

Cassie put her menu down. "You don't have to."

Luke closed his menu and let out a long, slow breath. "I don't want to leave, Cassie, but I can't imagine spending another night at your place without spending it in your bed."

Cassie bit her bottom lip and looked up at him from beneath her lashes. "I'm not worried about that anymore."

That must have been some storage room talk. Luke's heart began to thud loudly in his chest.

"But," Cassie started and Luke's hand clenched on the table, "I don't want to believe this is anything more than it is. That's what will hurt. Stay with me during your vacation. Then go back to New York. No expectations. No explanations needed."

Luke frowned. He told himself he should be happy. It wasn't the first time he'd been offered something temporary and casual. Women could often be just as blunt as men in this modern age. He usually applauded their frankness. This time however, he wanted to shake the woman saying it. "Didn't you say that was exactly what you didn't want?"

She shrugged, but didn't meet his eyes. "I changed my mind."

"Cassie, look at me."

When she raised her eyes to his it wasn't lust he saw in them, it was an emotion that twisted his gut. She would let him into her bed, but that was as far as she would trust him. He wanted more. "That's not good enough."

Her eyes burned with an emotion akin to anger. "What do you want?"

He took her hand in his and laced his fingers through hers. He searched for the words to describe how he was feeling.

A waitress appeared at the end of the booth. "Are you two ready, or are you still deciding?"

"All I know is what I don't want," Luke said, not taking his eyes off Cassie.

"I said yes," Cassie answered, sounding defensive.

"I'm getting a hotel room."

"Um . . . I'll just give you a few more minutes," the waitress said before retreating.

Cassie's fingers tightened on his. "I don't understand you."

Luke raised her hand to his lips and kissed it. "What do people in this town do when there is this much snow?"

"Do you mean like going to the movies? Bowling? Like a date?"

He rubbed her fingers back and forth across his bottom lip, while imagining how her soft lips would feel circled around his shaft. "Yeah, like a date."

"I'd like that," she whispered.

"What?" he asked huskily.

"Whatever you want to do." Cassie's lips parted and her eyes warmed with desire.

He leaned across the booth and pulled her forward until their lips almost touched. "You're not making it easy on me, Cupcake. Tell me what you want."

She licked her bottom lip. "I only know what I don't want, and that is to not know what it could have been like with us."

"I'll just pack you up something to go," the waitress, who had returned without being noticed, said.

Neither Luke nor Cassie so much as spared her a glance. Luke was lost in Cassie's eyes and had an inner debate between what he wanted to do and what he thought he should do. "I don't want to rush you. I want you to want this as much as I do."

Cassie closed her eyes for a moment as if gathering her strength and said, "I already do."

He kissed her across the table, feeling as excited as he had before his first date in high school. With Cassie, everything felt new. "Then what are we still doing here?" He helped Cassie into her coat and quickly threw on his own.

"Are we going bowling?" Cassie asked as they walked out of the restaurant. She tossed her car keys to him, and the wink she gave him was just about the sexiest thing he'd ever seen.

He held the passenger door of her car open for her and growled softly in her ear, "If that's what you want to call it."

"So, no hotel?"

It was a coy question that didn't require an answer. Luke sprinted around to his side of the car.

Chapter Six

CASSIE WAS GLAD Luke had decided to drive back because her hands were shaking with a mixture of excitement and nerves. They tried to make light conversation, but the sexual tension between them was too much to sustain a topic.

They walked into her kitchen together; the mounting anticipation was palpable. Cassie didn't realize she was hanging onto the doorknob until Luke gave her a curious look.

"We don't have to do this if you're not ready, Cassie," he said gently.

She'd felt brave in the restaurant and excited on the drive, but now, back at her place, she was nervous. "I am. At least I think I am. It's just been a long time."

He caressed the side of her neck lightly with one hand, and she sucked in an audible breath. "How long?"

His touch sparked flames of desire through her. She closed her eyes and savored the feeling before answering in a whisper, "Four, maybe five years."

She opened one eye and peered up at him to assess his

reaction. His expression was difficult to discern. "You don't remember?"

Cassie turned her head away. "I was lonely, and he didn't matter. I didn't even know his last name. I'm not proud of who I was back then. I wasn't in a good place."

Tenderly, Luke turned Cassie's face back toward his. "Don't hide from me, Cassie. You can tell me anything."

Cassie blinked back tears. *Unless I tell you I may be pregnant. I can guarantee that would be a mood breaker.* "Why am I so nervous? It's not like I'm a virgin."

He unbuttoned his coat, lifted her hand, and placed it on his chest above his heart. "You're not my first either, Cassie, but can you feel that? My heart is beating like I just finished a sprint. Do you know why? Because unlike every other time, this feels different—like I've been waiting my whole life for this moment."

Cassie's hand shook against his chest. His heart, like hers, was indeed beating a wild dance. "We barely know each other."

He placed his other hand over hers on the doorknob. "We can fix that." He gave her that lopsided, boyish grin of his that melted her heart. Again. "But you'll have to let go of the door, Cupcake."

She laughed nervously and did. He took her hand in his and brought it up to his mouth, kissing the inside of her wrist while never breaking eye contact with her. "Let's go upstairs to your room. We don't have to rush. I want to make love to you slowly, learn every inch of you, and watch you come again and again for me."

He swung her up in his arms and carried her out of the kitchen, up the stairs, and into her bedroom as if she were precious to him. Cassie buried her face in his neck and clung to him. His consideration for her almost brought her to tears. She was used to people who took from her. Even if he left before she woke in the morning, she wouldn't regret choosing to be with him. He wasn't like the fumbling boyfriends she'd had in high school, or the selfish short-term lovers she'd experienced as an adult. He was a man who knew how to please a woman and intended to enjoy doing that.

He eased her down onto her feet beside her bed. She brushed against his erection briefly, and they both shuddered. Ever so slowly he unbuttoned her coat before dropping it to the floor beside her. She reached for the belt on his jeans, but he stilled her hands. "Not yet. You first."

He kissed her neck and then each new inch of skin as it was exposed while he unbuttoned her blouse. Her shirt floated to the floor. With one hand he released the clasp of her bra and tossed it on the floor in the growing heap of clothing. He gently cupped each of her small breasts in his hands. "You're perfect. So beautiful."

"So are you," Cassie said huskily.

With his eyes burning with desire and his hands worshipping her, Cassie felt truly beautiful for the first time in her life. He circled a thumb around one of her puckered nipples. "I could come just from the sight of you." He gave her a droll look and added, "I won't, Cupcake, but I love that I could."

Cassie ran her hands over the bulging muscles of his shoulders and up to his strong neck. She arched backward and offered herself to him. With a groan, he lowered his mouth to one of her breasts and savored it. Cassie's body clenched with pleasure, and she was quickly wet and ready for him. He didn't rush, though. He teased her with his teeth. Flicked her with his tongue. When she was clinging to him and moaning, he took her into his mouth and sucked gently while rolling her other nipple skillfully between his fingers. When she thought she could take no more, he started all over again on the other breast. Cassie heard herself making sounds of encouragement she'd never made before. She'd never been a vocal lover, but sex had never been like this.

He turned her around, exposing her bare back to him. He took her ponytail and swished her hair back and forth, following the teasing path with his lips. His hot mouth rained kisses on her neck and spine. While kissing her shoulder, he reached around and unsnapped the front of her jeans. One of his hands returned to knead a breast, while his other slid beneath the front of her silk panties and cupped her sex. "You're so wet, Cassie. So wet for me."

"Yes," she answered, too lost in how he was making her feel to say anything more.

He slid a finger between her lower lips and began to slowly caress her clit. Cassie gripped a bedpost to steady herself. He took his time, leisurely learning what drove her wild. When he found it, he kept his rhythm steady and his touch sure.

Cassie rubbed back and forth against his bulging erection, loving how it felt even through their clothing. He continued to kiss her neck and shoulder, whispering how beautiful she was as his caresses drove her closer and closer to climax.

Just when she thought she was about to come, he withdrew his hand and turned her. She cried out softly. He chuckled softly at her expression. "Not yet, Cupcake. Trust me."

Wild with a need to finish what he'd started, she pushed his mouth up to hers. The kiss instantly deepened, and they feverishly began to remove the rest of each other's clothing. She couldn't get enough of him.

He picked her up and laid her in the middle of her bed. He knelt beside her and handed her a condom. She eagerly rolled it onto his cock. He was so big. So hard. She wanted him inside her with a desperation unlike anything she'd felt before. She spread her legs wide, wantonly, and parted her lips. *Take me,* she begged silently.

He bent to claim her mouth again, and his hand returned possessively to her sex. He stroked it firmly then once again began to caress her nub. In half the time, she was wild and nearing release. She ran her hands over every inch of him she could reach. Craving more. He increased the speed of his touch and slid his middle finger inside her. His tongue fucked her mouth while his hand sent her over the edge of climax and then through an explosive orgasm.

She shuddered and mewled into his mouth. Her ragged breathing heated their kiss more. When she calmed, he positioned himself between her legs. Cassie dug her hands into his back. She couldn't wait another second for him to be inside her.

But she had to.

He loved her by his rules. Once again he kissed her neck, her breasts, and teased her by sliding his cock back and forth against her wet slit. He nipped her breasts. Teased them. Returned to kiss her deeply on the mouth before moving to her shoulders and breasts again. All the while, dipping just the tip of him between her slick lower lips, sliding it back and forth across her clit until she was bucking upward and begging him to take her.

She cried out his name when he finally entered her. She was more than ready for him, and he filled her deeply. She spread herself wider for him, and he raised himself above her, watching her expression while he thrust into her.

His powerful claiming was primal, and she sensed the moment he lost control and began pounding into her with the same desperation she had welcomed him with. Time stood still. There was only the intense pleasure from their joining, the sound of their passionate breathing, and the lust in each other's eyes that neither could look away from. They were connected beyond their physical bodies. In that moment he was hers, and she was his; nothing else mattered.

They rode toward release together, almost violently. She dug her hands into his hair as his speed increased, and gave herself over to an orgasm she felt from her toes to the roots of her hair. He gasped, "Oh, baby, I'm coming," and thrust deeply one last time.

Still inside her, he gave her a long, tender kiss that blurred Cassie's vision with tears. When he raised his head he smiled down at her, and Cassie couldn't help but smile back. No matter what happened, she wouldn't regret knowing this side of him.

He rolled onto his side, disposed of the condom, then pulled her into his arms and kissed her lips softly. "I knew we would be this good together. I wanted you from the first time I stepped into your kitchen. You had a smudge of frosting on your face, and I wanted to lick it off you. I wanted to lick every inch of you, Cupcake. And I will. Over and over again. All night long."

Frosting? Baking. Cassie sat up. "Oh, shit. I have to bake for tomorrow."

He traced her collarbone then cupped one of her breasts firmly. "That's okay, I'll help you."

Smiling down at him, Cassie asked, "What do you know about baking?"

He slid his hand down her stomach and cupped her sex possessively. "Enough."

Suddenly breathing heavily again, Cassie whispered, "I can't let just anyone in my kitchen. What are your qualifications?"

His eyes narrowed with pleasure. He raised a hand to her breast. "A strong need to lick frosting from your tits." His talented fingers slid from her breast to her thigh. "Your thighs." His fingers slid to up her sex. "Then have you come in my mouth. I want to lay you across that table and taste every inch of you until you're begging me to fuck you."

I could come again from just imagining it.

"You're hired," Cassie said with a chuckle.

ONCE AGAIN DRESSED in jeans and a T-shirt, Luke leaned a hip against a counter and watched Cassie check on a batch of cookies in one of her industrial-sized ovens. Her hair was pulled back, but still wet from the shower they had shared. She looked sweet and innocent draped in her large apron. Even after the marathon day of sex they'd had, he felt his cock stir again as he watched her. "You have a smudge of blue on your neck," he said huskily.

She smiled at him playfully from beneath those naturally long lashes of hers and swatted at him with an oven mitt. "That's because you distracted me in the shower."

A wide smile spread across his face. Being with her felt right. He couldn't explain why or begin to guess what it meant for either of them, but he wanted to remain in this place with this feeling as long as he could. "I tried not to, but you had frosting in places I couldn't help but want to taste again."

She blushed. The timer on the oven went off; she pulled a hot pan out and slid it on a cooling rack. "You could make yourself useful and decorate the cooled batch." Their eyes met for a hot moment. "It's not like you don't know how to apply frosting."

A wave of warmth swept through him as he remembered how he'd drawn sugary trails along her body and then his own. Every touch, every flick of his tongue or hers was forever seared into his memories. No matter what tomorrow brought, he knew this time with Cassie would stay with him always. He dutifully picked up the pastry bag and began to pipe frosting on a cookie. "This is something I never imagined myself doing."

A small crease appeared between Cassie's eyebrows. "You don't actually have to do it. This part is probably boring for you. You're used to saving lives, not deciding between jelly beans or sprinkles for toppings."

He laid the bag down and pulled Cassie into his arms, looping his hands behind her back. "Hey, I'm enjoying this."

There was sadness in her eyes when she looked up at him. "Today. I bake every night. It's how I pay the bills in the winter. How long will it take you to get bored with this?" *With me?* She didn't ask the question out loud, but it was there in her eyes.

He pulled her to his chest and rested his chin in her hair. "You think we're so different, don't you? Too different. I'm not so sure. I don't claim to have had the type of childhood you did. I was raised with a nanny and cooks who took care of me. I was never hungry or alone. But my family was . . . is . . . classically dysfunctional. We used to eat entire meals together without saying more than ten words to each other. Talking to any of them is still often awkward. I accepted it because I didn't know anything else. Your life here is nothing like that."

She hugged her arms tightly around his chest. "What are you saying, Luke?"

He tipped her head back so he could look into her eyes.

"I want to spend this week with you. All of it. I don't care if we bake every night." Flashes of their prelude to baking brought a lusty smile back to his face. "In fact, I like the idea very much."

"Then you go back to New York and your life there?"

He wanted to say that wasn't how the week would end, but he'd never experienced anything like this before. He didn't know if something that felt as good as being with her could last. "Cassie . . ."

She raised a hand gently to his lips. "Don't say it. It's okay. I'm a big girl. I'll be fine."

Her words twisted through his gut painfully. He didn't believe in things like love at first sight or happily ever afters. He was a man of science, and in his experience, statistically, very few interpersonal relationships had the potential of working out long term. He knew all of that, but what he couldn't explain to himself was why the idea of leaving her made him feel physically sick.

Chapter Seven

FOUR DAYS LATER, Cassie and Luke were driving back from running some errands. Luke was driving with one hand and holding hers with his other. They were laughing and sharing funny anecdotes from their childhoods. They'd swapped injury stories and were working their way through their most embarrassing teenage moments.

They'd spent every night making love, every day working together on renovation projects at her bed and breakfast, and each evening baking. A couple of the orders had taken longer than normal to finish, but the quality of the interruptions had placed a perma-smile on Cassie's face.

According to Bonnie and Tilly, Luke was smitten. Both of them told Cassie they'd be shocked if he left at the end of the week.

Cassie couldn't allow herself to imagine anything more than a week with him. He wasn't staying, so there was no need to tell him about her possible condition. She'd double-checked with the clinic to make sure sex was safe and, because of the natural method she'd chosen for insemination, it was. There was nothing to feel guilty about.

Just because it wasn't forever didn't mean it couldn't be wonderful.

A car ran through a stop sign. Luke slammed on the brakes and put an arm out in front of Cassie to stop her from lunging forward.

A loud crash brought an instant halt to their conversation. A car had slid across the icy street into oncoming traffic and hit another head-on. Luke looked down at her quickly and said, "Call 911." He took off in a run toward the vehicles.

Cassie did, quickly stating their location and what had happened to the operator who answered as she rushed to Luke's side. "Okay, I'm at the car."

"Are you alone?" the operator asked.

"No, I'm with Dr. Andrade."

Luke had opened the driver's door of one of the cars and was checking the pulse of the woman who was slumped behind the wheel. Her airbag hadn't deployed, and she was bleeding profusely from her nose and mouth.

"She's barely breathing," Luke said urgently, as he unbuckled the woman and pulled her out of the car. A small crowd was gathering. One man threw his coat on the ground and Luke laid the woman down on it. He placed his ear to her chest.

The driver from the other car kept saying loudly, "Is she okay? I hit a patch of ice. I tried to avoid her."

Luke waved the man away, but he kept circling and asking about the woman.

Cassie told the 911 operator they needed an ambulance

and that one of the drivers was seriously injured. She put the call on speakerphone and said, "Luke, she wants to know how seriously."

In what Cassie could only assume was his authoritative physician voice, Luke said, "There is significant swelling around the woman's mouth and nose. Respirations are difficult and getting worse. Something is compromising her airway. I can't tell if she has any other injuries yet, but her nails are beginning to turn blue. How long until an ambulance gets here?"

"Seven minutes," the operator said. "Maybe ten. They're pulling out now."

"We don't have that kind of time," Luke barked. "She's non-responsive. We're losing her." He looked around the crowd. "Does anyone have a click pen?"

The man who had been hovering handed Luke one with shaking hands. "Is she going to be okay?"

Luke continued to address the 911 operator. "Tell the EMTs I'm performing a cricothyroidotomy. I have to get that airway open." He felt around the base of the woman's neck then pressed the pen down firmly on it until it broke through the skin.

Cassie looked away for a moment, then forced herself to look back. As soon as he'd broken through the skin, he removed the pen, unscrewed it, and replaced part of it to allow air into the woman's trachea.

Luke brought his face down next to the pen. "Respiration has resumed. How far out is the ambulance?"

"Three minutes, sir."

Luke opened the woman's jacket and checked for bleeding, then sat back on his heels. The crowd around them was growing and an ambulance siren could faintly be heard down the street.

"She's going to be fine," Cassie said to the circling man.

"How do you know?" he asked in desperation.

"Because she has one amazing doctor on her side. He won't let her die." Luke had taken off his coat to cover the woman. When the ambulance arrived, he spoke to the EMTs while they rolled the woman onto a board and lifted her onto a stretcher. As they stabilized the woman, Luke took a cleansing cloth from them and began to clean himself up.

Just before they closed the door, one said, "She's lucky you were here, Dr. Andrade, or she wouldn't still be with us."

The police took statements from everyone then took the driver who had crossed the median in for further questioning.

Cassie and Luke walked back to her car. Cassie reached for Luke's hand. "That was amazing."

Luke shocked her by pulling away. "It wasn't."

He was angry, and Cassie needed to understand why. "You saved that woman's life."

Her words only seemed to upset him more. "Yes. I saved a complete stranger. But when it comes to people I care about? I fail. Every time." He started to walk away from her.

Cassie grabbed Luke by the arm and swung him around. "What are you talking about?"

He rubbed his forehead roughly. "It doesn't matter."

SOMEWHERE ALONG THE WAY

Something told Cassie it did. It mattered just as much as anything else they had shared that week, maybe more. "Is this about Emma? Do you blame yourself for that?"

Luke grabbed Cassie's upper arms tightly. "I could have made her look into other treatments, but I didn't. I shouldn't have trusted her specialists when they said she was improving."

"You weren't her doctor anymore."

"But I was her friend."

Cassie winced. "You're hurting me."

His hands loosened, but he didn't release her. His eyes burned with a fury he'd turned inward. "The way you looked at me back there when I was working on that woman? Like I could save the world? That's not me. Emma would still be here if—"

"Or she wouldn't be. No matter what you did," Cassie answered angrily. She'd driven herself nearly mad wallowing in "if" questions when she'd first walked away from her mother. *If I'd begged her one more time to get help . . . if I'd let her stay with me one more time . . . maybe I could have cleaned her up.* For a long time, Cassie had blamed herself for everything just like Luke was doing, and she didn't like remembering that feeling. "You're not God, Luke. What I saw back there was a doctor doing his best to save a woman's life. If she had died, would that make you less a hero? Sometimes shit happens, Luke. Awful shit that we have no control over. You can beat yourself up over everything that might have been, or you can pick yourself up and go on. That woman is alive because of you. I'd say her family is pretty damn happy you were there. Don't tell me how I should or shouldn't think about anything."

The fight went out of Luke. He pulled Cassie to him and wrapped his arms around her. She hugged him and they stood there, simply holding each other for several minutes. "You scare me, Cassie. How do you look right through everything else and see me?"

Cassie tightened her hand on his and smiled up at him sadly. "Maybe we're not that different after all."

✧   ✧   ✧

LUKE KNEW SOMETHING was wrong that evening when the kitchen filled with smoke billowing from one of the ovens, even though Cassie was standing right beside it. After helping her fan the room out, Luke put his arms around Cassie's waist and hugged her from behind. "What are you thinking about?"

Cassie leaned back into his embrace. "Bonnie called earlier."

"And?" Luke asked, unable to resist a brief nuzzle of her neck.

Cassie reached back and buried her hand in his hair, a sure sign their proximity was giving her equally heated thoughts. She let out a shallow, half-excited breath. "She reminded me her restaurant was having a fundraiser dinner for the Scott family, and I'd promised to go."

Luke ran a hand up Cassie's leg, raising the skirt of her dress as he went. He traced the lace at the top of her panties before sliding his hand beneath them. Her hand fisted in his hair, and she rubbed her ass back and forth over his already raging hard-on. He tickled her ear with a hot breath and asked, "Is that a problem?"

With one finger he began to circle her clit slowly, loving how quickly she got wet as he did it. With his free hand he reached around to the front of her blouse and, with one strong move, tore it open. She closed her eyes and arched backward. He caressed her breasts through her thin silk bra. Cassie loved a gentle first touch that got rougher as they both became more excited. He enjoyed the same.

"Not a problem," she said, as if she could barely remember what they were talking about. "She just wanted to know if I was bringing you."

He didn't stop his caresses even as he asked, "Are you?"

With her eyes closed and her breath ragged with desire, Cassie said in a whisper, "Do you want to come with me?"

He slid a finger deep inside her, pumping it in and out while continuing to tease her clit with his thumb. "Always."

She writhed and moaned with pleasure. "I mean to the dinner."

He tightened his hold on one of her breasts as he continued to plunge his finger in and out of her wet sex. "Do you want me to?" he asked huskily.

"Oh, God, yes."

He chuckled and nipped her earlobe. "Then just ask me. Tell me what you want." He paused and waited.

Cassie spun in his arms, and pulled his mouth down to hers. She was deliciously forward as she drove her tongue into his mouth and ground her body against his. Their kiss was wild and hot. Like a storm that raged through both of them, sweeping away each other's desire to speak. She undid his belt and took his cock into her hands. Luke leaned back against the kitchen table and groaned as she fell to her knees in front of him and took him deeply into her mouth.

Her lips were heaven. Her tongue circled and teased. She cupped his balls with one hand and pumped her mouth up and down on him until all coherent thought left him. He watched her until pleasure made it impossible, and he was wildly near release.

She rolled a condom onto him. Beyond caring about anything except having her, Luke forcibly swept the table behind him clear of bowls and utensils. He leaned back, pulling her forward to straddle him.

She knelt above him, then lowered herself onto him, throwing back her head with a cry as she moved up and down, taking him deeper each time. They rolled on the table, laughing as they almost fell to the floor. He withdrew, adjusted his position so he could stand beside the table, and held her hips as he drove into her. He leaned forward, slid an arm beneath her, raised her so she was clinging to his shoulders, and then lifted her off the table.

Her hands were everywhere on him. He was mindless with his need to take her further, drive himself deeper within her. She met his thrust with an animalistic eagerness.

When they came, it was loud, sweaty, and left them both shaking, intimately connected as they both came back to earth. After several days of sex with Cassie, Luke would have thought things would be cooling between them, but it was even more intense because they were learning what brought each other the most pleasure.

Slowly, reluctantly, they disentangled from each other. They arranged their clothing the best they could and laughed as they picked up the bowls Luke had knocked from the table.

Still flushed from her orgasm, Cassie stacked the bowls in the sink. "I'm going to be baking late tonight."

Luke joined her at the sink, kissing her slightly swollen lips softly. "I'll help you."

Cassie chuckled. "You're not as much help as you think."

He pushed her hair off her neck and trailed hot kisses from her ear to her shoulder. "Are you complaining?"

She blushed and shook her head. "Not at all."

Her question from earlier came back to him and he said, "The fundraiser dinner sounds like fun. Count me in."

Cassie tensed beside him. "It's next Thursday. Won't you be gone by then?"

Luke froze. They hadn't spoken about his departure date. Honestly, he'd put it out of his head and for once had just enjoyed being in the moment. His vacation had originally been for one week, but he had cleared his schedule. He didn't have to return to New York yet. "I don't have to be," he answered simply. "I could stay longer."

Cassie turned to pin him down with those beautiful brown eyes of hers. "You mean for another week?"

He didn't have an answer for that. "I didn't expect to meet someone when I came here, Cassie."

Cassie's forehead furrowed with irritation. "Well, I certainly didn't expect you, either."

He pulled her tense body into his arms. "Tell Bonnie I'll attend the dinner with you."

She pushed against his chest. "Maybe you shouldn't. Maybe we should keep to our original plan."

He kissed her forehead gently and continued to hold her. "None of this was part of my plan, but I can't walk away from you."

"Yet," she said angrily.

Another man might have lied to her and spouted promises he didn't intend to keep. That had never been Luke. "Whatever happens, I would never intentionally hurt you. If you want me to leave now, say so, and I'll go."

She beat both of her fists on his chest in frustration, then grabbed the front of his shirt, went up on her tiptoes, and kissed him boldly, wantonly on the mouth. "One more week. That's all you get. I can't give you more than that."

Yet, Luke thought, but kept it to himself. Instead, with all the pent up emotion within him, he kissed her. She kissed him back hungrily, and her baking didn't get done until early the next morning.

Chapter Eight

"I NEED YOUR advice," Cassie said into her cell phone as she paced the floor of her bedroom two mornings later.

"Okay, okay, calm down. What happened?" Bonnie asked urgently.

Cassie waved at the collection of dresses she'd strewn across her bed even though she knew Bonnie couldn't see them. "I should have said no."

"To what?" Bonnie asked again, sounding like she would have shaken Cassie if she'd been in the same room.

"To a date with Luke today. He said he wanted to take me somewhere and said I should wear something nice. I don't know what that means. I don't go anywhere. I don't have fancy dresses." Cassie sat on the edge of her bed. "I'm going to tell him I feel sick because that's not a lie."

"Stop," Bonnie said firmly. "You do have nice dresses; I've seen you in them. Maybe they aren't designer brands, but men don't care about that. I would come over, but I promised I'd wait at the restaurant for the plumber who's supposed to fix the back sink that's always leaking. Go turn on your laptop so we can Skype. I'll hop on the computer in the office."

Cassie turned on her laptop and felt even more ridiculous when she was face to face with her friend. "I'm sorry to bother you with this, Bonnie."

"Are you kidding? I love this stuff. Do you have a little black dress?"

Cassie put the laptop down on her bureau and returned to hold up a dress in front of the camera. "Like this?"

Bonnie shook her head. "Something without a turtleneck and long sleeves."

"I have a blue dress I used to wear when I'd go out dancing. I don't even know if it still fits me." Cassie held up the dress for inspection. "Isn't it too cold to wear something like this?"

"Trust me, I doubt you'll be outside long." Bonnie looked it over critically. "I have to see it on you."

Cassie moved away from the camera eye, stepped out of her robe, and into the dress. She reluctantly walked back in front of the laptop. The dress felt shorter and tighter, and it didn't cover nearly as much of her cleavage as she remembered. "I don't think it fits anymore."

"Turn around." Bonnie made an evaluative sound. "Are you wearing underwear?"

Cassie blushed. "Of course."

"You need to wear a thong under a dress like that."

"I don't own any."

"Then go commando."

Cassie shook her head. "No way."

Bonnie rolled her eyes. "Which would you rather do?

Look like you're wearing your grandmother's undies because that dress shows everything, or wear nothing and possibly give Luke a thrill on the way home?"

Cassie turned in front of her bedroom mirror and grimaced at the very obvious panty lines she saw. "I guess you're right."

"I am. That's the dress you should wear on your date. You look amazing."

Cassie stepped out of her underwear and gave her backside another look in the mirror. "I don't know if I'm sexy enough for it."

Bonnie waved a finger at Cassie. "A woman is as sexy as she feels. Own it, and you'll rock it."

Cassie nodded and made a soft affirmation to herself. "Own it."

"What are you planning to do with your hair?"

Cassie usually threw it back in a ponytail. She shrugged. "Down?"

"Definitely. And shoes?"

Cassie held up a strappy pair tentatively. "These?"

"Perfect."

Cassie put on the shoes and spun in front of the mirror. "I think I can do this."

"I know you can. Cassie, Luke already likes you. You're going to turn him on just by showing up. Don't worry."

Cassie walked over to the laptop and bent down in front of it. "If you were here I would hug you, Bonnie. You have no idea how much better I feel."

Bonnie looked over her shoulder and said, "That's what

friends are for, Cassie. Anytime. Hey, I think I hear the plumber knocking on the door. I have to run. Good luck, and tell me all about it when you get back."

Cassie closed the laptop with one hand and straightened. She felt silly being worried about going out on a date with Luke after she'd spent over a week sleeping with him. But this was something new. This took them out of her home and into the actual world. Somehow that made what they were doing feel real, and that scared her.

Real relationships hurt when they end.

And don't fool yourself, Cassie, this is going to end.

She carefully applied makeup and blew out her hair until it shone in thick, long waves down her back. She chose small, simple gold earrings and left her neck bare. Better to have nothing there than something that looked cheap.

I'm ready.

Well, as ready as I'll ever be.

She picked up a matching clutch purse and stepped out of her bedroom. Luke was already in the hall. He was in a nice suit that reminded her of the first day she'd met him. Sophisticated. Expensive. From a completely different world than she was. She raised her chin and repeated Bonnie's words in her head. *Own it, and you'll rock it.* She walked confidently toward Luke. "You look nice."

A smile tugged at his lips. It was the sexy smile she was familiar with, which was usually followed by him sharing a naughty idea. *Or two.* "You look almost too good to take out, Cupcake."

Still not sure she wanted to go, she said softly, "We don't

have to go anywhere."

He closed the distance between them and gave her a short, sweet kiss that shook her as deeply as any they had shared. "We do. You work hard. You deserve to be pampered. Come on, let me spoil you today."

She laced her fingers with his. "Are you going to tell me where we're going?"

"Do you have any problem flying in a small plane?"

Cassie's eyes rounded. "Not that I know of."

His smile widened. "Then no. I want to surprise you."

"You told me to pack a small bag, so I canceled my orders for tomorrow and the next day. I didn't know what time we'd be back."

He stopped halfway down the stairs and pushed her back against the banister for a deep kiss. "I like the way you think." One of his hands ran up her bare thigh and beneath the back hem of her dress. When he encountered the bare skin of her ass, he gave it a healthy squeeze then raised his head and growled, "I *really* like the way you think." He brought his other hand around, cupping her ass in his strong hands. He groaned. "We need to leave now while I can still walk."

Knowing she had the power to push him out of control was an aphrodisiac like none other. Cassie wrapped her arms around his neck and pressed herself against him, loving the desire she saw flaring in his eyes. "You're right, we don't want to be late for whatever you have planned."

He groaned and began to kiss her neck deliciously. Cassie arched against him. He lifted her up in his strong arms, carried her back into her bedroom, and laid her out on her bed. With a sexy chuckle he said, "They'll hold the plane."

✧   ✧   ✧

TWO HOURS LATER, an overnight bag hastily packed and carried on, Luke and Cassie were seated side by side in a single-engine Cessna 206 as it circled a private airstrip adjacent to endless rows of grape vines, trimmed short and blanketed in snow. "Welcome to the Blue Heart Vineyard, named after a diamond desired by the wife of the previous owner. They never had children. Possibly because the wealthy man gave his wife one hundred eighty acres of wine country instead of the thirty-carat rock Harry Winston was selling at the time."

"It's beautiful."

"I'll tell Noah you like the place. He and his wife bought it about three years ago. You'll like JoAnne. She was shy when we first met her, but she's come around."

"We?"

While appreciating the view out the window and reminiscing, he absently answered Cassie. He'd told himself he would go to see Noah's new place as soon as things slowed down at work and with his family. Three years had passed. The realization weighed on Luke's mood. "I was there the night Noah met her. He dragged me to a dreadfully boring charity garden party his mother was hosting. I was supposed to be his excuse to leave early. Then he saw JoAnne and the rest is history. They've been inseparable since. I haven't seen them much since they left New York, but I still consider them two of my closest friends."

"Oh, my God," Cassie said softly as the plane descended to the airfield below.

It was then Luke heard the distress in Cassie's voice. He turned and noticed Cassie had gone pale and took her hand in his. "Landing in a small plane can be a little unnerving in the beginning, but it's perfectly safe."

She chewed her bottom lip, her eyes wide with worry. "You didn't tell me we were visiting friends of yours."

Was she worried what they'd think of her? Luke bent, gave her a kiss on the cheek and said, "Don't worry, Cassie, they'll love you."

Cassie shook her head back and forth in strong denial, then she blurted, "You don't understand."

The level of her concern was unexpected. He'd chosen to bring Cassie to meet his friends because he'd wanted to demonstrate to her she was more than a casual vacation hook-up. He'd assumed she'd be pleased. He wasn't sure how to interpret her reaction. Anyone who could run a bed and breakfast would surely not be shy when meeting new people. "I don't."

She looked away from him as if debating how honest she wanted to be with him. She turned back to him and blurted, "I'm still not wearing underwear. I didn't even bring any. It was so much fun before, and I thought we'd be alone. I can't meet your friends like this."

The plane touched down on the runway with a series of soft bumps. Luke tried, but couldn't contain his amusement. Cassie's admission was both enchantingly innocent and so hot he was sporting another hard-on. It was a condition he was becoming accustomed to around Cassie. She looked so embarrassed that he laughed out loud, and laughed harder when she frowned and smacked him on the arm.

"This isn't funny."

He wiped tears of mirth from beneath his eyes. "Cassie, you have no idea how good it feels to be with you."

She glowered at him for a moment more, then a corner of her mouth turned up with a reluctant smile. "You could at least pretend to sympathize."

He tried to look contrite but gave up and simply grinned down at her. "The one I feel badly for is me. How am I going to concentrate on anything but you now with that image in my head?"

"You knew I was commando back at my house."

"I know, and look what happened there."

They shared a long look at the heated memory. He pulled her to him for a brief kiss. "Seriously, if you're not comfortable we can leave now and come back. But say it now because I believe they're heading down the walkway to meet us."

Cassie glanced out the window of the small plane to confirm what he'd said. "We can't leave now. What would they think?"

Luke turned Cassie so she was looking at him again. "I don't care what they think. I care how you feel. Are we staying or going?"

She made a face at him and said, "I don't mind meeting your friends. I just don't want—"

"Them to see your assets," Luke finished and chuckled again.

She waved a finger at him. "You will pay for this."

He caught her hand and brought it to his lips. "We'll see. Noah said we could use his guesthouse. I'm confident I can win your forgiveness there." He slid one hand up the bare expanse of her thigh to the hem of her dress. "I'll apologize all night long if you want, Cupcake. Would you like that? I'll—"

The side of the plane opened, and a cold gust of air whipped into the cabin. Cassie gasped and clamped her knees together. "Man, that's cold."

Luke barked out another laugh and helped her to her feet. He couldn't remember a time when he'd felt as light-hearted and free. If she'd honestly been upset, he would have turned the plane around and left, but he was glad they were staying. Bringing Cassie to meet Noah and JoAnne felt right, just as being with Cassie felt right. It was a simple truth that Luke was beginning to question less and less.

Chapter Nine

"**W**OULD YOU LIKE me to take your coat, ma'am?" a man in a dark blue suit asked Cassie.

"No, thank you, I'll keep it on," Cassie answered. She glanced at Luke who was handing his coat to a member of the staff and silently dared him to say a word.

Cassie had only spoken a few words of greeting to JoAnne when she'd met her out by the plane, but she could understand why Luke's friend had fallen for her so quickly. She was stunning. Perfectly tailored in woolen pants and a delicate matching sweater, JoAnne was intimidatingly put together and sophisticated. She wore her jet-black hair in a sassy, modern bob, which complemented her delicate features and mocha complexion. Everything about her screamed cultured elegance, but her smile was openly friendly and sincere.

Cassie took several deep, calming breaths.

JoAnne's husband, Noah, was a tall man, with beautifully dark skin and jet-black eyes. He was dressed in dark gray trousers and a sweater Cassie guessed had cost more than any dress she'd ever owned. He carried himself with an easy confidence that likely came from being born with money. *I don't belong here.*

Still, it was hard not to like Luke's friends, especially after seeing the heartwarming hug Noah had exchanged with Luke. They were two men who had known each other long enough to consider themselves family.

Luke had brought Cassie forward and introduced her simply as, "This is Cassie Daiver."

Cassie's head had spun with questions. Luke had said it as if he'd mentioned her to them already. She wanted to know what he'd told them. While at the same time, she wasn't sure she did.

They'd quickly made their way to the main house to get out of the frigid weather. Now that they were all gathered inside, Cassie couldn't help but take a moment to appreciate the beauty of their home. She was fairly certain her entire bed and breakfast could have fit in the main foyer. A beautifully ornate staircase curved off to one side, accented with paintings Cassie guessed were originals.

There was nothing tacky about the home, but it sent a clear message. Luke's friends were wealthier than anyone Cassie had ever encountered.

Questions bubbled within Cassie, undermining her confidence. *What would these people think of me if they knew how I grew up? I probably still make less each year than their house staff. Would they care if they knew?* She thought about the dress she was wearing and how little it had cost and was even more reluctant to remove her coat.

"Are you cold?" JoAnne asked in a sweet tone.

"No," Cassie answered honestly, then cursed herself for jumping on that reason to retain her coat. "I mean, it's my fault if I am. I didn't dress appropriately."

"I noticed," JoAnne said with a small smile.

Cassie swallowed hard. "You did?"

JoAnne pointed to Cassie's feet. "As soon as I saw your strappy pumps I guessed Luke didn't tell you where he was taking you. Poor thing. He probably thought he was being romantic, but what he actually did was make you traipse through the snow practically barefoot. Men." She looked Cassie over from head to toe. "I'm shorter than you are, but if you'd like to borrow anything warmer than what you have on, don't hesitate to ask."

Cassie choked back a nervous laugh. There was no way she was asking for the one item she regretted not wearing the most. "Thank you. I wore a sleeveless dress. I don't know what I was thinking."

JoAnne called out softly, "Mia, please bring in a tray of coffee and tea." Then she turned and spoke to Noah and Luke who were happily catching up. "Why don't we move into the library? Noah, have Brimlow make a fire. We don't want to freeze our friends out of wanting to go on your tour."

"Good idea," Noah said before waving over the man who had taken their coats. "We'll be in the library, Brimlow."

"Yes, sir," the man answered as he headed into the room and began to prepare the fireplace.

The atmosphere was formal and more than a little intimidating.

JoAnne led the way to a circle of chairs beside a large fireplace. She waved for Cassie to choose one and sat in the one beside her. Within moments there was a hearty blaze of logs burning with a tray of warm beverages and desserts laid out for the two couples.

Luke stood with Noah on one side of the fireplace. "Do you remember what we used to do at your grandmother's house?"

Noah wrinkled his nose. "You mean throw whatever we didn't want to eat into the fire and hope no one would notice?"

"You didn't," JoAnne said in amused reprimand.

Luke laughed. "It was Noah's idea. He hated anything with mushrooms, and his grandmother's chef loved to hide them in the most unlikely dishes."

Noah joined him in laughing at the memory. "I believe it was the time I threw a large cut of lamb that Grandmother demanded I clean the ashes out myself."

"You made such a mess, Manny started stashing food for us out of pity for the house staff." Luke walked over and sank into the chair beside Cassie. "Manny was Noah's male nanny. How old were you when your parents finally let him go, Noah? Twenty?"

JoAnne leaned toward Cassie with a huge smile spreading across her face. "I love when these two get together. I always learn something new about my husband. Noah, did you really have the same nanny for twenty years? My mother worried I'd get overly attached if any of mine stayed too long. I always envied the children who were close to theirs."

Noah winked at Cassie. "I'm on my best behavior today because you're the first woman Luke has brought around for us to meet, but don't worry, I have plenty of good stories to share with you."

Luke took one of Cassie's hands in his as if it were the most natural thing to do, and those gorgeous dark eyes danced with amusement as he said, "Don't believe a word he says, Cassie."

Cassie was torn with how she felt. On one hand, she couldn't relate at all to their shared experiences. But, strangely, she didn't feel as out of place as she would have thought she would. Luke's friends were welcoming her into their circle.

After asking Cassie if she'd like some, JoAnne poured Cassie a cup of coffee and handed it to her. "Are you originally from Ohio, Cassie? I lived in this area when I was young, but then my family moved to New York. Moving back here was the best gift Noah has ever given me."

Cassie hesitated before answering. She met Luke's eyes and saw nothing but encouragement there. "I grew up in Michigan. Actually, Detroit, Michigan. I live in Defiance, Ohio, now." Cassie held her breath. A thousand possible awkward questions they could ask circled in her mind. She told herself it didn't matter what Luke's friends thought of her.

JoAnne's expression didn't change. She handed her husband a cup of coffee and said, "Luke mentioned that you own a bed and breakfast. I knew I would like you the moment I heard that. It takes a special kind of person to deal with the public. We give tours in the summer, and I get so nervous I forget everything I'm supposed to say." She laid a hand on her forehead softly in embarrassment. "I've had people ask me if it's my first day on the job."

With a mischievous twinkle in his eyes, Noah said, "Don't worry, sweetheart, so far only one person has suggested I fire you."

JoAnne arched her head back and laughed at Noah. "And what did you tell them?"

The smile he gave her was mischievous. "I told her the truth. Your job is secure, only because I'm sleeping with you."

JoAnne waved a hand in the air. "Did you really say that? I hope you also mentioned we're married."

"How would that have been fun?" Noah asked comically.

JoAnne playfully swatted the air in his direction.

Cassie laughed softly at the warm exchange.

JoAnne met Cassie's eyes and said with mock sternness, "Cassie, don't encourage him."

Noah went to stand behind his wife, put a hand on both of her shoulders, and kissed the top of his wife's head. "If you're actually cross with me, perhaps we can make up later."

Luke barked out a laugh. "Oh, how marriage has tamed you, Noah."

Noah raised his head and looked pointedly back and forth between Luke and Cassie. "Laugh all you want, Luke; I have a feeling we'll soon see what it does to you."

Luke's mouth opened, then shut without saying a word.

Cassie's hand shook so hard she spilled coffee on her

jacket. She dabbed at it with a napkin, while avoiding meeting Luke's or anyone else's eyes as she did.

No one spoke for a few long moments, then JoAnne suggested cheerfully, "Noah, how about we give them a tour of the winery now?"

✧   ✧   ✧

LATER THAT NIGHT, Luke hugged a naked Cassie to his side beneath the thick plush blankets of the vineyard's guesthouse. Her eyes were closed, although he knew she wasn't asleep. Her breathing was deep and relaxed, and her lips were slightly curled in sated pleasure. He kissed her forehead gently, and her smile widened. "See, not having underwear worked out for the best after all."

She rubbed her hand over his chest softly. "I'm too relaxed right now to be able to argue that point with you."

He chuckled. "Imagine how relaxed you would have been if you'd taken more than a sip of that ice wine. I think I'd like you tipsy."

Cassie tipped her head back and opened her eyes lazily. "You have a one-track mind."

"Only with you," he said, realizing how true it was. He'd been with other women and enjoyed it, but if someone had told him that sex could get better the more you had it with the same person, he wouldn't have believed it. Familiarity led to a deeper comfort, not normally this fiery connection that exploded every time he touched Cassie.

She kissed his shoulder. "I want to believe that."

He cupped her face with one hand. "I've never lied to

you, Cupcake, and I never will. I grew up in a house of secrets and half-truths. I have no tolerance for either."

She tensed against him. "Sometimes people hold things back because there's no reason to burden the other person with it."

He knew she meant well, but he didn't need her to defend his family. Just the thought of the drama that waited for him back in New York was enough to threaten his good mood. "I haven't found that to be the case, but let's talk about happier things. Noah and JoAnne really like you."

Cassie looked as if she was about to say something important, then changed her mind. The smile on her face appeared strained for a moment. Luke cursed himself for allowing his frustration to take away from what was otherwise a wonderful night.

She laid her head back on his chest with a sigh. "Your friends are great. And the way they talk about their winery . . . it's hard to believe they've been doing this for such a short time."

"They found something they were both passionate about. My only regret is that it took me so long to come out to see them. This is the happiest I've seen either of them."

Cassie closed her eyes again and let out a shaky breath. "It's obvious how much they mean to you."

"They do," Luke said as he tried to put his feelings into words. "It was important to me that you meet them and they meet you."

Cassie shuddered against Luke, but she kept her eyes firmly shut. Luke traced his hand up one of her arms and tucked a lock of hair behind her ear.

"I've been doing a lot of thinking today, Cassie."

Her eyes shot open at that. "Don't say it, Luke."

He pulled her tighter against him. "Why does the idea of anything developing between us scare you so much? When I watched my friends together today and saw how happy they were with each other, I asked myself if I'd ever been like that with anyone. The answer was yes—you. When I'm with you, Cassie, I don't think about everything in my life that's wrong. I'm myself, but different. You make me laugh. You make me think. I don't want to imagine a night without you in my bed. There. I've said it. I don't want to put an end date on what we have." Cassie's eyes burned with an emotion he couldn't understand. She looked cornered by his declaration, and he suddenly felt like a boy who grabbed a part of a sandcastle only to feel it slip away between his fingers. "Talk to me, Cupcake."

Her hand fisted on his chest. "You don't get to change the rules in the middle of the game."

Luke frowned. "I'm not playing a game. Are you?"

She brought her hand up to her temple and gave it a nervous tap. "No, of course not. That's not what I meant."

"Then what?"

Tears misted her eyes. "I've always considered myself a brave person, but when it comes to you . . ."

He kissed her lips, stopping her from saying more. "It's okay, Cassie. I won't rush you. I just want you to know that my side of this is decided. I'm not going anywhere."

Her visible nervousness brought out his protective side.

He rubbed her back and murmured for her to go to sleep. Meanwhile, he told himself to do the same before he made all sorts of ridiculously premature declarations.

She was a wreck just because he'd suggested he wanted to stick around.

How would she react if he told her the truth—he was falling completely, irreversibly, in love with her?

Chapter Ten

LATER THE NEXT day, back home and alone in her room, Cassie sank into the chair beside her closet and stared down at her cell phone. She'd sent Luke to the store for a few items and was glad she had when she'd received the call a few minutes earlier from the fertility clinic. She hadn't picked up. She'd just sat there, letting it ring through to voice mail.

She gathered her courage and hit the button to play the message. "Good morning, this is Toledo Fertility Clinic reminding you about your ten a.m. appointment tomorrow. There is no need to call unless you have an issue."

An issue?

Is that how anyone would describe what feels like the verge of a mental breakdown?

She forced herself to listen to the message again. *It's time to stop pretending I didn't have artificial insemination. This is what I wanted. This is the reality of what I chose.*

It was the first time Cassie wasn't sure if she wanted her results to be positive, and that realization shook her. *Why wouldn't I want to be pregnant?*

Because of Luke?

No matter what he said, what are the real odds he'll be here a year from now? Even a month?

Too vividly, Cassie remembered the cycle of hope and then the days of disappointment that had followed her two earlier treatments. Nothing had been more important than having a baby.

Until Luke.

What if I find out I'm pregnant tomorrow?

She wiped away tears she hadn't realized had fallen.

What if I find out I'm not? She stood, walked into her bathroom, and splashed cold water onto her face. She felt sick, but she doubted it was morning sickness. No, her gut was twisted with an emotional turmoil she'd bought upon herself.

Should I tell Luke everything today?

Or wait for the results of my test tomorrow?

If I'm pregnant, will telling him send him running back to New York?

And, if I'm not, what do I tell him then?

The chime of a doorbell rang through the house. At first Cassie thought she'd imagined it, but it rang again. *Oh, great. I usually pray for paying guests, but not today.*

Cassie sprinted down the stairs and opened the front door. A short brunette smiled and stepped inside. She started talking before Cassie had a chance to ask her who she was.

"I hope you don't mind me dropping in like this. I'm looking for Luke Andrade. I heard he was staying here."

Cassie's stomach did a painful somersault. *Please don't let this be his wife.* "Are you a friend of his?" Cassie asked.

"I'm his cousin, Maddy."

Cassie closed her eyes for a moment as relief swept through her. "He'll be back in about an hour if you'd like to wait."

The woman looked at her watch. "That should work. I told my husband I'd be home tonight."

More good news. She wasn't staying. "May I take your coat?"

Maddy shrugged off her coat and handed it to Cassie. Cassie had the strangest feeling the woman was sizing her up as she returned from hanging the coat up. "Are you hungry? I have some blueberry scones. They're still warm."

"That would be lovely," Maddy said.

"I'll bring some out to you if you'd like to sit in the living room."

"I don't mind the kitchen, if it's easier. You don't need to go to any special trouble for me." She took out her phone and sent a quick text. "Although if you have an extra one, I'll run it outside to Gino. He's unhappily waiting in the car for me."

"Your boyfriend?"

"Bodyguard."

"Oh," Cassie said as she led the way to the kitchen. She wrapped a scone in a napkin then poured hot coffee into a paper cup and handed them to Maddy.

Maddy headed outside with it and returned, shivering. "I should have kept my coat on. Yikes, it's cold out there."

Cassie placed a mug of steaming coffee and another plate

on the table. "This should warm you up."

Maddy sank her teeth into the scone with a happy sound. "Delicious. Did you make this from scratch?"

"Yes. I love to bake."

"You'd get along well with my husband. He's a chef with an impeccable palate, but I can say with confidence he would love this."

"Thank you," Cassie said.

After taking another bite, Maddy wiped her mouth delicately and turned her attention to Cassie. "So, you're Cassandra Daiver?"

The way she said it made Cassie's hair rise on her neck. Maddy sounded as if she had information about her. Cassie told herself she was being paranoid. Most likely what Maddy knew was what everyone in town knew... Cassie owned Home Sweet Home. "My friends call me Cassie."

"It's a beautiful name."

"Thank you," Cassie said, feeling at a loss for what else to say, but knowing she was repeating herself.

"And Luke has been here for almost two weeks?"

Cassie ran a dishrag over the counter beside the coffee pot. "I don't feel comfortable giving out information about my guests."

"Of course," Maddy said simply and took another sip of coffee. "Have you owned this place long?"

"Two years."

"Must be a lot of work for one person."

Cassie shrugged. "It is, but I enjoy it."

An awkward silence stretched between them. Cassie

straightened up her kitchen absentmindedly. Maddy nibbled on her pastry.

"May I be blunt?" Maddy asked, breaking the silence.

"Sure," Cassie answered. She had a feeling her permission or lack thereof wouldn't sway the other woman one way or another.

"I'm worried about Luke. He and I have never gone more than a couple days without speaking. He wasn't himself before he left New York. I understood when I heard a friend of his had died, and he was flying out here for the funeral. I wasn't worried at first, but the hospital told me he cleared his schedule of patients until further notice. He's never done anything like that before. No matter how upset he is, he can't keep hiding out here. Just tell me, is he okay?"

Cassie clasped her hands in front of her to stop them from shaking. She didn't want to think Luke was using her as a way of hiding from his life. She didn't want to think about Luke at all while the little brunette was scrutinizing every one of her expressions. "I really can't speak for him or his state of mind."

Maddy frowned. "I understand." She tapped a finger on the table beside her plate. "You and Luke aren't . . . together, are you?"

Cassie put a nervous hand up to her hair and turned away. "He's a guest here. That's all."

Softly, Maddy said, "It would be okay if you were. It would actually explain a lot."

"We're not."

Maddy nodded and sighed. She turned and opened her

purse. She turned on her phone and asked, "Would you like to see a photo of my husband? This is his 'stay out of my kitchen' expression."

Cassie crossed over to look at the photo. She couldn't help but smile when the man's expression seemed to say exactly that. "I can imagine many chefs feel that way."

"Did Luke tell you he has three brothers? Want to see them?"

Cassie sat down across from Maddy. "Sure."

Maddy showed her a photo of Luke and three other men, and Cassie spoke without thinking. "That must be Gio. He does look stern. Nick is exactly as I imagined. And, Max, off to the side and independent just like Luke said. Isn't it funny how family photos capture so much?" Cassie stopped talking when she realized she'd said more than she'd meant to. She hastily added, "I heard Luke describe them once."

Maddy didn't look like she believed her, but she didn't say so. She swiped her phone a few times, then held out another photo. "This is me with my husband, Richard, and our two sons. The older one is Joey. The little one is Adam. I feel badly every time I leave them, but thank God for private jets, you know what I mean?"

"Not really," Cassie said absently. She couldn't take her eyes off the photo. It might have been the love in Maddy's and her husband's eyes as they looked at each other. Or the way the children were laughing on their laps. They were happy children who had two parents.

In that moment, Cassie imagined herself in similar photo

with Luke. No matter how unrealistic it was to hope anything that had started the way their relationship had could end up like the calendar-perfect family in the photo, Cassie couldn't deny how much she wanted it to.

She covered her eyes and burst into tears.

Maddy gave her hand a light rub. "Oh, no. No crying. I was just trying to find out more about you. I didn't mean to upset you."

"You didn't," Cassie said, even as tears continued to run down her face. The clinic had told her the hormones she was taking to help with fertility could make her more emotional, but it hadn't been a problem during her first two cycles.

"My cousin Nicole says I'm an emotional ox at times. I'm so sorry."

Cassie covered her face with her hands. "It's not you. It's me. I fucked everything up. Absolutely everything."

"I'm sure it's not all that bad."

Cassie continued to cry. "Yes, it is. It's very bad."

Maddy went to stand beside Cassie. She put her arm around her. "Okay, well, my father always says that problems are simply situations awaiting solutions. So, whatever you did, I'm sure we can fix it."

Only because she had kept her secret inside her so long it was tearing at her to be released, Cassie said, "If I told you something, could you keep it to yourself?"

Maddy's hand stilled on Cassie's back. "Yes."

"You were right; there is something going on between Luke and me. But it's not going to work out because I didn't tell him I may be pregnant," Cassie said, feeling a weight lift from her chest just by saying it aloud.

"Is it his?" Maddy asked.

"No," Cassie said and stood. She walked over to a box of tissues, took one out, and blew her nose.

✧   ✧   ✧

WITH HIS ARM full of groceries, Luke knocked on the kitchen door with his elbow. Every muscle in his body tensed painfully when he saw the distressed expression on Cassie's face. He quickly placed the bags on the counter and took her face in his hands, wiping the remaining tears from her cheeks. "What happened?"

He looked past her and a deep anger began to build within him as he began to piece together what had upset Cassie. "What are you doing here, Maddy?" The contriteness in his cousin's eyes only fed Luke's temper. He stepped between Cassie and the person he was beginning to believe he had spent far too much time defending.

Maddy put out a hand in appeal toward Luke. "I was worried about you. I know why you came here. I wanted to make sure you were okay."

Luke looked down at Cassie's red and puffy eyes and said slowly, "Are you okay, Cassie?"

Cassie raised a hand to her lips and fresh tears spilled over. She shook her head, but she didn't say anything.

He turned back to Maddy and snarled, "Did you upset Cassie?"

Maddy's mouth dropped open. She was used to being indulged, excused. She looked lost for what to say. Well, it was about time she learned she couldn't crash through other people's lives as she pleased. Finally, she said, "If I did, it wasn't my intention."

Luke advanced on Maddy. "Cassie, could you give me a moment alone with my cousin?"

Cassie laid a gentle hand on Luke's arm. "It's not what you think, Luke. It's not her fault."

With a reassuring pat to Cassie's hand, Luke said, "You don't have to make excuses for Maddy. She makes enough for herself."

Cassie appealed to Luke one more time. "Luke, don't let me come between you and your cousin. She's here because she cares—"

Luke gently ushered Cassie toward the door. "We'll talk when we're alone, Cassie. I promise. What I have to say to Maddy has been a long time in coming. I'll explain it all to you later."

Cassie lingered at the door for a moment and gave Maddy a look Luke didn't know how to interpret. The moment she was out of the kitchen, Luke rounded on Maddy again. She was giving him the apologetic eyes that usually won her forgiveness. This time, however, Luke saw it for the manipulative act it was. "How well would you say we know each other, Maddy?"

Maddy clasped her hands in front of her and swallowed visibly. "Well enough for me to recognize that you are really, really angry with me."

Luke slapped a hand down on the counter beside him. "Do you know how many times I have defended you? When our families split, I stayed in contact with you. These past few years, all I've done is encourage my family to accept you, even when I saw how you bulldozed into their lives."

Maddy squared her shoulders. "Sometimes love needs—"

Luke pushed off the counter. "Don't spout that shit to me. You think you've helped my brothers? Brought us closer? I'd say their temporary truce is despite you. Without you, my mother wouldn't have gone after Julia. She wouldn't have been able to threaten Rena. Every time I hear of a problem in my family, and I dig for how it started, I always find you, Maddy. You."

Maddy took a step back, shaking her head. "It's not like that."

Luke advanced. "Hard to hear the truth about yourself, Maddy? Isn't that what you say everyone needs? The truth? Tell me, that journal you wanted me to read, what did you do with it? Because if I know you, you couldn't keep it to yourself. You can't stop meddling, even when no one wants your help. Even when we tell you to stop."

"Lies are what kept our families apart. The truth will—"

"I'm done making excuses for you. It's time for you to grow up and realize that sometimes things are none of your fucking business. I don't know what you said to Cassie, and I don't care about your version." He slowed his breathing, controlling his temper, even though fury was raging within him. "You don't belong here. This place, what I have with Cassie, I won't allow you to sully it. Go home, Maddy. Give me time to forget how angry I am with you."

Maddy opened her mouth then closed it with a snap. "I

didn't mean to upset Cassie."

"But you did."

With an emotional shine to her eyes, Maddy said, "You're like a brother to me. I would never do anything to hurt you or anyone you care about. I love you."

Not softening his stance, Luke held her eyes and warned, "Then prove it. Stay the hell out of my relationship and keep your damn secrets to yourself. I don't want them, Maddy. I'm happy here."

Maddy nodded slowly as though she were processing his request sadly. "I hope everything works out for the two of you."

"It will," Luke said with determination. "I found the woman I want to spend the rest of my life with."

"Oh," Maddy said vaguely. She looked about to say more then bit her lip. "I should probably head back to the airport. Richard is expecting me home tonight."

Luke nodded and unfolded his arms from across his chest. He didn't like that he'd hurt his cousin with his honesty, but he considered it something she'd needed to hear. He walked with her to the living room where he retrieved her coat and handed it to her.

Cassie stood off to the side of the room, looking nervous and more than a little sad. Luke tensed when Maddy walked toward her. He strode over, prepared to cut Maddy off if she said anything more than goodbye.

Maddy shook Cassie's hand. "Good luck, Cassie. I'm deeply sorry if my visit upset you."

Cassie looked from Maddy to Luke and back. "Thank

you."

"Take care of him for me, Cassie," Maddy said, and with one last sad look at Luke, she let herself out the front door.

Luke took Cassie into his arms. She was shaking with emotion, and he simply held her for several moments. With a tearless sob, she wrapped her arms around his waist and buried her face in his chest.

Finally, Cassie raised her head and said, "We need to talk, Luke."

He picked her up, carried her into the living room, and sat down with her still in his arms. He rubbed his chin gently back and forth in her hair. "Yes, we do."

Cassie laced her fingers through his. She was breathing quickly, and he wanted to spare her from whatever she was about to say, but he sensed she needed to let it out. "Remember when I told you I'm much more messed up on the inside than you know?"

Luke nuzzled Cassie's ear and said softly, "We all are."

She squeezed his hand tightly. "I have something I need to say, but before I do, I want to tell you a story. I want you to understand why I am the way I am."

"I'm listening, Cassie. And you can tell me anything."

"When I was young I didn't know how bad my home life was. I thought everyone's mother left them alone as much as mine did, had strangers in their own homes, had to hide whatever they didn't want stolen from them. I thought everyone grew up afraid."

Luke stopped breathing. In that moment his heart opened even wider for the woman in his arms. "Oh, Cupcake . . ."

She played with a button on his shirt, focusing her eyes there. "I've never told anyone, but I think it's time I say it out loud."

If Luke could have, he would have done anything to erase whatever had put that tone in her voice, whatever had hurt her so badly she couldn't look at him while she spoke of it. He had an idea, but he didn't want to believe anyone could have ever hurt the beautiful woman in his arms.

"I didn't know him. He was just someone my mom brought home from wherever she'd been partying. I was used to strange men coming and going. Normally they didn't even look at me. As if by acknowledging me, they acknowledged something they didn't like about themselves. I wasn't even really afraid when my mother passed out, and he came to talk to me."

Tears were running freely down Cassie's cheeks, but she didn't wipe them away. She kept her attention glued to one white button. "I was ten. I almost don't remember everything that happened. I remember being scared. I remember trying to get away, but he pinned me down on the couch . . . and then pain. He left and I lay down next to my mother. I tried to wake her, but I couldn't."

Luke knew that such horrors happened in the world. He'd volunteered in a shelter when he was in college. But nothing had ever cut him as deeply as hearing Cassie retell what had happened to her. He wanted to erase it from her, but he knew enough to understand she needed to remember. Her experience, however ugly, was a part of the woman he loved. He remained quiet, letting her choose how she'd tell the rest.

"I told my mom the next day. All she did was cry and go on another drug binge. Like somehow my pain was too much for her. I knew I couldn't tell anyone else. Kids in my neighborhood were taken away from their parents for less. They didn't always end up somewhere better. And I loved my mother, even though I hated what she did." Cassie looked away and dried her eyes. "I remember pulling deeper inside myself, so deep no one could hurt me. I was scared. And then, somehow, I wasn't anymore. I was numb. I created these hiding places in my neighborhood where I could go whenever my mother brought someone home. I stole whatever I needed. It was never good, but I was okay. I was surviving. As long as I never trusted anyone. As long as I kept to myself, hiding and protecting everything that was important to me."

Luke continued to rub Cassie's back as she spoke. "You don't have to hide anymore, Cassie. Not from me."

"I want to believe that, Luke. It's like when I first heard Emma speak of this town. How they were like a family to her. I couldn't imagine living anywhere like that. Maybe I didn't think I deserved to be part of something that good. But I wanted to be part of that. I wanted it so badly." She rubbed a hand across Luke's arm absently. "People in this town care about me. I'm not afraid here, not even of the people who stay in my home. I'm strong. I shed the person I was in Detroit, and I'm becoming someone else . . . someone better."

Luke took her hand gently in his. "Not someone else. You, Cassie. That's all. This is who you really are."

Cassie closed her eyes for a moment. "I still have trouble trusting anyone, and I hide what I care the most about. There are things I don't tell Bonnie. Things I haven't told you, yet. I want to, but I'm scared."

With his heart thudding loudly in his chest, Luke continued to hold Cassie. She'd never been more beautiful to him than she was in that moment. "Don't be afraid with me, Cassie. You are the bravest, most warmhearted woman I've ever met. There is nothing you could say that would change my opinion of you." He let out a long breath and admitted, "I'm in love with you."

She didn't say she loved him back, and he didn't expect her to. She wasn't ready yet. He ran a comforting thumb back and forth over hers. She had opened herself up to him, leaving herself vulnerable. He wanted to show her he was willing to trust her just as completely. "Cassie, I can't begin to understand what you've been through, but I do know what it's like to feel powerless. My mother didn't physically hurt us, but she was unpredictably vicious. There was so much anger in our home. We all dealt with it in different ways. I convinced myself I could heal them. That's why I became a surgeon, I think. I had this crazy idea that I alone could make things better for everyone. The nurses in our hospital call it the god complex. Men who begin to see themselves as being able to overcome even death itself. But no one is that powerful. I couldn't fix my family, Cassie. I couldn't save Emma. I wish I could go back in time and protect you from everything you described, but I can't. All I can do is tell you I'm here now, and I'm not going anywhere."

Cassie opened her eyes and looked up at Luke. "Maddy said she was worried you were hiding here. What if you are? You could wake up tomorrow and miss New York."

"Is that what you're afraid of? Maddy doesn't know what she's talking about. New York is just a city. Concrete buildings. Obnoxious traffic. Yes, my job is there, but I could be a surgeon anywhere. Even here."

Cassie buried her face in Luke's chest, and he tucked her head beneath his chin. Cassie had shared a part of herself with him she'd never shared before. He saw that as the precious gift it was. She had more she wanted to say, and he knew she would—in her own time.

Cassie didn't trust easily, and she would love even more cautiously. Luckily, patience was a virtue he'd been born with.

Chapter Eleven

"**W**HAT IS YOUR problem?" Bonnie asked, after waiting until they were alone in the bathroom of her restaurant.

Cassie washed her hands in the sink, using the action as a distraction. She didn't meet her eyes in the mirror above it, and she wasn't about to meet Bonnie's. There were probably a hundred, maybe a thousand better ways to handle how she felt, but none were possible for her. Since she'd left the fertility clinic the day before, she had gone numb. "I don't have a problem."

Bonnie folded her arms across her chest. She was absolutely lovely in the shimmering green dress she'd chosen that night and normally Cassie would have said so, but nothing felt real. It was as if Cassie had taken a step back from her life and was unemotionally watching it play out below. "Oh, you do, and you will tell me what it is. You're here tonight with the most eligible bachelor who has ever come to Defiance. A man who, might I add, is obviously smitten with you. You look amazing, but I haven't seen you smile once since you came in. Luke hasn't left your side, and if I had to guess, he's just as worried about you as I am. He doesn't appear sorry, just confused. Did you two have a fight? Spill it. What's going on?"

Cassie turned on the water and was about to wash her hands again when Bonnie turned her away from the sink. "Look at me, Cassie. I've never seen you like this. Whatever happened, you're not alone. Talk to me."

A woman walked into the bathroom and glanced at the stalls. "Are they free?"

Bonnie scooted the woman right back out of the bathroom. "No, they're not. Come back in a few minutes." As soon as the woman was clear of the door, Bonnie closed it and slid a lock across the top. "Now, we can do this the easy way or the hard way."

Cassie looked up and hated that she was handling herself so poorly. Bonnie was missing part of the fundraiser she was hosting to hide out in the bathroom with her. She tried to force a smile. "There's nothing wrong, Bonnie. I just have a headache."

Bonnie nodded and stepped closer. "I'm sorry to have to do this."

Cassie raised an eyebrow in question.

Standing within a foot of Cassie, Bonnie stared, unblinking, into her eyes. "I will now awkwardly stare at you until you can't take it anymore and tell me what I want to know. My father used to do this to me. Don't doubt the power of a prolonged, knowing stare."

One corner of Cassie's mouth twitched. "You're serious?"

Bonnie didn't budge; she just continued to stare into

Cassie's eyes. At first Cassie brushed it off as ridiculous. Then annoying. Then she felt more and more uncomfortable. Cassie shifted from one foot to the other. "Stop."

"I will, as soon as you start talking."

"I already told you there is nothing to tell." Cassie looked away but could still feel the pressure from Bonnie's sustained attention. She rubbed one of her ears nervously and tried to pull back the wretched feelings beginning to surface within her. She couldn't hide, not even from herself, beneath Bonnie's unwavering scrutiny. "Fine, I received some bad news. Or maybe it was good news. I don't know. It just put me in a funky mood, okay?"

"From your mother?"

"No. I don't talk to her."

"I know. And that's probably for the best. You don't have to tell me what she did. I know you well enough to know you have a huge heart, Cassie. If you closed a door on someone, they earned it."

Cassie looked up at the ceiling and blinked a few times. *Hold it together, Cassie. No more crying.*

Bonnie's voice softened. "So it's not your mother. It can't be anything Luke did. You don't look angry. You look sad, Cassie. You've told me several times you moved here because you wanted to be part of a community. You wanted friends. Well, this is what happens when people love you. We can't stand to see you hurting. We get all up in your business and don't let go until we know you're okay."

Cassie let out a long, sad breath. "I'm not pregnant."

Bonnie took a few moments to process that announcement. "Was there a reason you were hoping to be?"

Cassie rubbed her cheeks with her cold hands and turned to look at herself in the mirror. "I've been going to a fertility clinic in Toledo for intracervical insemination or IUI. I didn't want to tell anyone unless I had good news. I found out yesterday this cycle didn't work any better than the first two, even though I used hormones this time. The clinic suggested I try a different donor or opt for a more invasive procedure."

Bonnie put an arm around Cassie. "Oh, sweetie. I knew you wanted a family. I didn't know how badly. My sister went the fertility route with her husband. I know how devastating negative news can be."

Cassie wiped away a stray tear. "You're not upset I didn't tell you?"

Bonnie met her eyes in the mirror and tucked hair away from Cassie's face. "Being friends doesn't mean we have to tell each other everything. There are no rules."

Cassie frowned. "Then what was all that staring about?"

Bonnie flashed a brief smile. "That was for your own good. And given the same situation, I would do it again." The two were quiet for a moment, then Bonnie asked, "Luke doesn't know, does he?"

Cassie shook her head and shrugged. "At first I didn't think it would matter. I never thought he would stay. Then I told myself it was better to wait until I knew something. Now I don't know what to say. I don't even know how I feel. You're right, I felt devastated the first two times the procedure didn't work. This time was different. I didn't cry when I got the news. I didn't feel anything at all. I still don't." She turned and took one of Bonnie's hands in hers. "What's wrong with me?"

"There is nothing wrong with you. Fertility hormones make women loopy. I'm pretty positive if you murdered someone while on them an insanity plea would work. My family was ready to have a 'please stop taking hormones' intervention with my sister by the time she finally got pregnant."

"I don't want to murder anyone."

"Well see, you're better than many already."

"The clinic asked me if I wanted to move forward with a different procedure. I told them I don't know."

Bonnie smiled. "And that surprised you?"

"I wanted a baby so badly. It was all I could think about for months. How could it not matter to me anymore?"

"Cassie Daiver, this is why you need to open up to your friends. You're driving yourself crazy with questions that anyone who knows you well could easily answer. You still want a baby, but now you want to raise it with one particular sperm donor."

Cassie's mouth dropped open. "Luke? He's going back to New York soon."

"Really?" Bonnie asked drolly. "I'll believe that when I see it. Sweetie, open your eyes. He is head-over-heels falling for you."

"Can you really picture him living here?"

Bonnie threw up her hands. "Hello? Yes. People love him already. He's gorgeous, nice to all the old ladies. Let's see, he also publicly saved Irene's life. Oh, and someone anonymously donated two hundred thousand dollars to our playground fundraiser tonight. Is there any doubt it was him? Yeah, I hate to imagine what our town would be like with him around." There was a knock on the door. Bonnie loudly told them to try the men's restroom.

"That's not what I'm saying. We may want him to stay, but what's here for him?"

Bonnie smiled confidently. "Us."

Cassie closed her eyes for a moment. "I feel sick every time I let myself start to believe he means anything he says. My hands get sweaty. I can't sleep. I can't eat. I've never had a panic attack in my life, but sometimes my heart races so fast I can't think. Is that normal?"

"That's love, sweetie. At least, in the beginning. It morphs over time. Work through this, and you'll enjoy the amazing honeymoon period. Savor that one because when the children do arrive there will be times when you want to smother him with a pillow while he sleeps beside you. My mother always said that's normal. It's usually because you're both sleep deprived. Add incessant snoring and the pillow smothering gets tempting. That's why Greg and I are waiting. I don't want to want to kill him yet."

"Bonnie, promise me you'll never become a marriage counselor."

Bonnie shrugged. "I didn't say you should smother him, I just said you may want to. If you fight that urge long enough, the kids grow up, move out, and the two of you live happily ever after together."

"According to your mother."

"Hey, she's been married to the same man for forty plus years. She knows her shit."

Cassie smiled reluctantly, then she sobered. "So, what do I do now? Should I tell Luke everything?"

Bonnie hugged Cassie again. "Maybe not here at the fundraiser, but soon. He deserves to know, don't you think? Love is hard enough. You don't want this to be what comes between you."

There was another knock on the bathroom door.

"What if I fall in love with him, and you're wrong? He just leaves?" Cassie asked, as much of a question to herself as to Bonnie.

"You're stronger than you think, Cassie. You'd survive." Someone banged on the door again and Bonnie sighed angrily. "Oh, for cripe's sake, we're coming out. Do all of you have the bladders of a two-year-old?" She took one last look in the mirror and asked, "How do you feel?"

Cassie's eyes filled with grateful tears. "Better than before you dragged me in here. Thank you, Bonnie."

Bonnie reached up to unlock the door. "The knowing stare. It never fails."

✧   ✧   ✧

WHEN CASSIE AND Bonnie returned to the dining room, Cassie was smiling. Luke sent Bonnie a grateful smile. Bonnie was a good friend to the woman he loved, and that made her one of his favorite people in the world.

Love.

The more he said it to himself, the less afraid he was of the truth. *I love Cassie Daiver. I love her in my bed, across the table from me at breakfast, by my side wherever I am. I love her when she's nervously snapping at me while we get ready for an event and when she's whispering naughty suggestions to me in the middle of the night. I want the side of her she shows me and the side she's still hiding. I want it all.*

Greg, Bonnie's husband, took a swig of his beer and also watched the two walk toward them. "You probably don't need my connections, but my brother knows a lot of local hospital administrators. He sells medical supplies. He might be able to put in a good word for you if you decide to stick around."

Luke gave Greg a grateful pat on the shoulder. The welcome the people in Defiance offered him had nothing to do with his enormous trust fund. In fact, he doubted they had a clue how wealthy he truly was. He didn't know if the way they treated him would change if they ever discovered the truth, but somehow he doubted it. The restaurant was packed with a variety of people from the community, from the bank president to the school custodian. They mixed and swapped stories as only people who had all grown up together in a small town could. He envied that closeness.

His cell phone rang. He groaned when he saw the number. It was his oldest brother, Gio. If he didn't pick up, Gio would only call again. If he ignored his call, Gio would likely fly out to check on him. All Luke wanted to do was figure out what Bonnie had said to Cassie to lift her mood, but it would have to wait. He kissed Cassie briefly on the cheek and held up his phone. "I hate to do it, but I have to take this. I'm going to step outside for a minute."

Cassie cocked her head to the side, but didn't ask.

Luke said, "It's one of my brothers. I'll be right back." He grabbed his coat from the rack beside the door, stepped out into the cold night air, and answered Gio.

Never one to waste time on pleasantries, Gio said, "Luke, Mother's in the hospital. We need you back here."

"What happened?"

"She had another one of her episodes, but this time, her nurse called an ambulance. She's not coherent, so I was able to bypass her doctor. But we may not have much time. The hospital is running routine tests. I want you to come back and look over the results. We can decide where to go from there."

Anger and frustration rose within Luke. "I went to see Mother before I left New York. She expressly told me to stay away from her medical records. She has a doctor, one she is comfortable with. Talk to him."

"He's not here; no one can find him. And even if he were, he wouldn't tell us anything. I'm starting to believe he's part of the problem. Get your ass on the next plane to New York. We'll talk about this in person."

"I'm not coming back, Gio."

"I'm having trouble hearing you. Did you just say no?"

"That's what I said."

Gio was quiet for a moment, then said, "Are you okay?"

"I'm fine."

"Did something happen that I don't know about?"

"No."

"This isn't like you, Luke."

"You're a big boy, Gio. If you want to get into Mother's medical records, throw some money at Dr. Garnert. He just weathered a divorce; he'll do anything for the right price. He's just as qualified as I am to diagnosis her. Probably more so considering whatever is causing what you call an episode is not my area of expertise. You don't need me."

"I spoke to Maddy a few days ago. She said she was flying out to Ohio. Did you see her?"

"Gio, I'm at a fundraiser tonight. If you want, I'll call Dr. Garnert for you. That's as far as I'm getting involved."

"Luke—"

Luke hung up his phone and stuffed it into the breast pocket of his suit jacket. He inhaled deeply and ran his hands through his hair. A month ago, he would have run to his mother's side. He would have poured over her test results and joined his brothers on what was sure to be an emotional rollercoaster full of drama and deceit.

The rush of concern and guilt he normally felt whenever dealing with his mother didn't come. Instead he asked himself what possible good could come from getting involved. His mother had denied his help vehemently, viciously. She'd called him a dog that came back no matter how many times she kicked him away.

Well, this time he wasn't rushing to her side. Her last kick still echoed too clearly in his head. And his brothers? They didn't need him. They had each other and their supposed soul mates in their lives. More recently, they also had more than enough support from their uncles and cousins.

Cassie was his priority now, and she was waiting for him. Luke turned and started to open the restaurant door when his phone rang again. Max? His youngest brother never called him.

"Luke, I just got off the phone with Gio. You need to come home."

Luke's eyes met Cassie's through the glass window of the restaurant. "I am home."

"Okay," Max said slowly. "He says he is home."

"Put him on speakerphone," Nick, Luke's other younger brother, ordered. "Luke, it's Nick."

"I know."

"You've got us all a little concerned."

"There's no need to be. I merely suggested Gio contact a colleague of mine who is a specialist in cardiology. He can determine how serious her condition is and recommend whatever treatment is necessary."

"See," Max said. "He doesn't want to come back. Luke, this isn't how our family works. I'm the one who takes off when shit like this happens. You're the one who rallies us together."

Nick asked, "Should I threaten to go out there and get him? It brought you home."

"I don't know," Max answered slowly. "I'm not that complicated. This is Luke. You know how intense he gets."

"I don't have time for this right now," Luke said impatiently. "I've made my decision clear. There are three of you there. You can handle this without me."

Nick joked, "Have you met us? Luke, this is serious. We need you."

Luke remembered a conversation Cassie and he had shared on the night of Emma's funeral. "It's time for you to figure out who you are without me."

Max swore. "I told you Luke took that woman's death hard. He's going to kill himself."

It sounded like there was a scuffle with the phone. Nick spoke next. "He's not going to kill himself. Luke, tell Max you're not considering anything like that."

"No matter what he says, I say we fly out there."

Luke clenched his phone in frustration. "I am not suicidal. I'm in love."

"Oh," his brothers said in shocked unison.

Max said, "Well, bring her with you."

"There is no way I'm exposing her to my toxic family, not like this."

In his usual mocking tone, Nick said, "I'd take offense to that label, but there's no denying we're an acquired taste. I would also promise we'd all be on our best behavior, but honestly Gio's already losing his mind. Max is only here because his fiancée won't let him leave. Maybe you're right. Maybe you should sit this one out."

"Oh, hell no," Max retorted. "If Luke gets to call out of this one, Tara and I are on the first plane out of here."

"Shut up, Max," Nick snapped.

"Just because you work with Gio doesn't mean you need to start sounding like him, Nick."

Luke closed his eyes and pinched the bridge of his nose. "If I thought I could actually do any good by returning—"

Max said, "Gio is buzzing in. I'm adding him."

Gio's voice boomed through phone. "Did you get in touch with Luke?"

"He's on the phone with us now," Max answered.

"Is he coming back?"

"No," Luke answered for himself.

"He's in love," Nick added dryly.

"Fuck," Gio said.

Nick joked, "That's congratulations in Gio lingo."

"What are we going to do?" Max asked.

Gio sighed. "Luke, whatever you have going on out there in . . . where the hell are you?"

"Ohio," Luke supplied, rolling his eyes skyward.

"It'll still be there a few days from now. Right now, you belong here with us."

Max interjected, "Don't make him say it. Please don't make him say it."

Gio continued, "We love you, Luke. And whoever you met and however she makes you feel, that hasn't changed. At times like this, family duty comes first."

Max groaned. "I have to talk Julia into easing up on pushing Gio to express himself. Am I the only one who still cringes every time he gets mushy?" A second later, Max said, "What was that for, Nick? Smack me again and see how that works out."

In an ironic tone, Gio added, "If you like having three brothers, don't make me sit in a waiting room alone with them. I'm only human."

Luke met Cassie's eyes again through the window and caved. "Okay. I'll fly back tomorrow morning. But only for a couple days."

His brothers all had something to say about it, but Luke had stopped listening. There was no amount of guilt or sense of duty that could convince him to risk what he had with Cassie by exposing her to the darker side of his family.

He was heading back to New York.

Now all he had to figure out was how to tell Cassie he was leaving and not taking her with him.

Chapter Twelve

CASSIE INTENDED TO talk to Luke after they left the fundraiser, but as soon as they entered her home, he swung her up into his arms and carried her up the stairs to her bedroom. The kiss he gave her was full of emotion as well as passion. It was an irresistible combination.

Slowly, tenderly, he unzipped her dress and let it fall to the floor at her feet. His hands cupped and worshipped her bare breasts. Cassie shivered with pleasure and started to impatiently remove his clothing.

They were soon both bare-chested, and Cassie reveled in the feel of his muscular chest beneath her hands. He had a way of touching her, holding her, that made her feel safe as well as desired. Luke was a man who knew what he wanted. He led her where he wanted to go, but made sure she was with him every step of the way.

He slid a hand beneath the lace of her panties and groaned with pleasure when she shifted so he could touch her more deeply. They continued to kiss even as Cassie undid his pants and pushed them down, freeing the evidence of how much he wanted her. He paused his intimate caress to help her step out of the last of her own coverings.

Naked before each other, they ran their hands over each other as they stood beside the bed. He took his time, tracing each of her curves. His mouth followed the tantalizing trail of his fingers. Cassie stroked his shaft with one hand while she greedily enjoyed the rest of him with her other. They had spent the last two weeks learning how to please each other, bringing almost unbearable intensity to their lovemaking.

She bent and took him into her mouth, loving how his hands dug into her hair as she went deeper. By now she knew just how to circle him, just how deeply to take him to drive him nearly out of control. His passion fed her own in a way that was new to her. His groan revealed he was close to release. Cassie would have continued to his climax, but he pulled her back up to face him and kissed her deeply.

They were both shaking with need when he picked her up and carefully tossed her on the bed with the sexiest smile she'd ever seen. He looked down at her as if she belonged to him, with him. Cassie wanted both to be true. She gave him what she hoped was an equally sexy look and beckoned him to her.

He sheathed himself in a condom then crawled across the bed to her and positioned himself above her. He settled himself between her legs, his thick, hard cock pulsing against the outside folds of her sex. Holding himself slightly above her with his elbows, he buried both of his hands in her hair. "Do you know how beautiful you are? Every inch of you. Inside and out. The more I have you, the more I want you. Give yourself to me, Cupcake. Give me all of you. Not only what you think I want. Don't just come with me, take me where you want to go."

Cassie pushed him off her and onto his back. His smile widened. Although they'd had sex many times, he had always been the aggressor, the one who set the pace. Cassie sat back on her heels and caught her breath in her throat. An idea had come to her, but she'd held back from doing it. She'd only read about it.

His eyes half closed with pleasure as if he could read her thoughts. "Do it, Cassie. Tell me what you want."

Trusting him as she had never trusted another, Cassie swung a leg over his torso and sat with her knees on either side of his head. It was in the asking she felt vulnerable. Others had demanded, and she had given. Luke had suggested, and she had enjoyed. But never before had she boldly taken her own pleasure. She raised herself, holding onto the headboard with both hands and brought her sex down to an inch above his mouth.

He cupped her ass with one hand as he worshipped her with his mouth. Cassie closed her eyes, still tense and unsure. Luke used his other hand to part her so his tongue had better access to her clit. He blew on it gently. Circled it. He ran his teeth back and forth across it until he found the pressure and caress that had her writhing against his mouth.

Self-consciousness fell away and Cassie moved with his mouth, opening herself wider to his tongue. She looked down, met his eyes, and used her hand to squeeze and tease her breast. She could tell by the way his hands gripped her that he was enjoying the display. She slowly dipped a finger into her mouth then used it to draw wet circles around her nipples. Luke moaned with pleasure and drove his tongue deeply into her. Cassie came with a freeing, uninhibited cry.

After a moment of readjusting, Cassie lowered herself down on Luke's cock, loving how he filled her. She closed her eyes, giving herself over to the feeling of being in control of their rhythm. As her speed increased, Luke swore and ground himself upward, his thrusts becoming as wild as she felt. When Luke came it was with a growl of satisfaction. Cassie's second orgasm rocked through her. Still above him, their intimate connection unbroken, Cassie smiled down at him. She was sweaty and trying to catch her breath, but she'd never felt more powerful or alive.

He ran a hand lovingly up and down one of her thighs. His eyes sparkled with warm humor. "I do believe you enjoy being on top."

She leaned down, holding herself above him with a hand on either side of his head. "Who knew?"

He wiggled his eyebrows suggestively. "I did."

Cassie grinned and said sassily, "Doctors: they think they know everything."

He grabbed her hips and rolled onto his side. She laughed as she fell onto the bed beside him. "Only because we do, but we don't usually brag about that to mere mortals like yourself." He whipped the bed sheets around them and pulled her into his arms. He nuzzled her neck and breathed her in as if her scent was also an intense pleasure for him.

In that moment Cassie felt her defenses crumble. There was no way to fake the feelings he was displaying. She didn't have to protect her heart from him. He wasn't going anywhere. It was time to tell him the final piece of her story. "Luke, I never thought it could be this good. I tried not to let you in so I wouldn't be hurt when you left. But now I—"

Luke cut her off, a frown creasing his forehead. "Cassie, there's something I have to tell you."

A cold panic tightened Cassie's chest. *Don't assume the worst. It could be anything.* "What?"

He rolled onto his back and sighed. "I'm flying back to New York tomorrow morning."

As quickly and as completely as her heart had opened to him, it slammed shut. His announcement fed every fear she'd had. It fit the pattern of her childhood. The people she let closest to her disappointed her the most. A familiar distancing numbness that had helped her survive the unspeakable in the past, filled her again as she cursed herself for believing for a moment he would stay. She didn't physically pull back from him, but she was already a million miles away in her head. "Will you want breakfast before you go?" she asked calmly.

He sat up, his frown deepening. "I wouldn't leave, but there's a family crisis that needs my attention. I should be back in a few days."

Self-doubt filled Cassie as she wondered if she had jumped too quickly to a conclusion. She remembered his brothers had called him. There could be something back in New York he had to deal with. She knew she had difficulty trusting people. Was this another example of that? She held the sheet to her chest and went up onto one elbow. "What kind of crisis?"

He rubbed a hand over his eyes in frustration. "My mother is in the hospital."

With that, Cassie sat all the way up. "Oh, my God. Is it serious?"

"It could be. She hasn't been in the best of health lately."

"Is that why your brothers called?"

"Yes, they want me to look over her records and make sure her doctors are doing all they can."

Cassie laid a hand on his chest. "I'm so sorry. Do you want me to go with you?"

He raised her hand to his lips and kissed it. "No. This is something I need to do alone."

Alone. His words cut through her. "Of course," she said, unable to keep coldness from her tone.

His hand tightened on hers. "What is going through that beautiful head of yours?"

She pursed her lips and chose an honest attack. "You don't want me to meet your family."

"You're right; I don't," he said, then seemed surprised when she pulled away from him and slid off the bed. He rose and stood beside her. Although they were once again naked and face to face, the emotions crackling through the air were entirely different. He took her arms in both of his hands. "You'll meet them one day but not like this."

And there it was, the truth about how he saw her. She wanted to yell at him: *You said you wouldn't do this. You said you wouldn't leave me. Please, don't leave me.* Cassie didn't say any of that, though. She held those thoughts inside and tried to distance herself from the pain. "What time are you leaving in the morning?"

"Early."

Cassie walked to the door of her bathroom, took her robe off the hook, and covered herself. She felt as if she were about to lose control. "I have orders to fill I didn't make earlier tonight. You should probably sleep in your room so we're both well rested for tomorrow."

Luke followed her and turned her in his arms. "Don't shut me out. I knew you'd be hurt when I told you, but I need you to trust me on this. It's better this way."

She struggled to pull away from him, but he held her before him. That alone triggered a violent response within her. She growled and began to swing at him with her fists. "Get your hands off me."

He instantly let her go. "Cassie, there's no reason to get upset. I'll be back in a few days."

Once the door to her past insecurities had opened, outrage that couldn't be suppressed flooded through her. With it came a wave of emotion from discovering she wasn't pregnant, all the guilt that had been building within her, and anger with herself for not being able to control how she felt. What she suddenly saw when she looked at him was a man who could undo all the good she'd brought into her life, and she couldn't let that happen. "No, you won't, because there is no need to."

Standing there completely indifferent to his state of undress, Luke said calmly, "I'll call my brothers. I'll tell them I can't go back yet."

Cassie held up two shaking hands in a plea for him to stop. What did it mean if he could change his plans that easily? Could it be that his mother wasn't even sick? "No. I want you to go. And you don't have to wait until morning to leave, Luke. I don't even want you to stay here tonight. Get out of my room. Get out of my house. Just—get out."

Luke made a gesture of appeal to her, but she recoiled from him. He picked up his clothes from the floor angrily and paused at the door. "I'm leaving because I want you to understand I respect you and what you've been through. It's not what I want, but it's what I'll do."

After closing her bedroom door, Cassie sank to her knees and covered her face with her hands. So many conflicting emotions stormed within her. In that moment she didn't know if she loved or hated Luke. He'd brought to the surface insecurities and fears she preferred to deny she had.

She listened to him open and slam shut the drawers in his room. She heard his footsteps approach her closed door and then it sounded as if he'd placed a hand on the other side of it. "I need to go back to New York because I told my family I would. But I am coming back, Cassie. And when I do, we'll talk this through."

Cassie closed her eyes tightly and didn't answer him. She wanted to believe him, but fear and her past held her immobile. She didn't move until she heard a car pull up to the front of her house and the door of her downstairs kitchen open and close.

He was gone.

✧   ✧   ✧

A FEW PHONE calls and several hours later, Luke stripped down to his boxer briefs and lay down on his own bed in his Manhattan apartment—alone. He rolled onto his side and punched the pillow by his head.

The quiet of his apartment was oddly depressing, and that realization was more than a little unsettling. Whether it was a woman he was sleeping with, or a family member he was visiting, he normally kept all of it outside of his apartment. It didn't matter how hectic or chaotic life was out there, his apartment had remained his tranquil, efficiently furnished retreat.

Luke rolled over angrily—again. He'd replayed his last conversation with Cassie many times during the trip back. He cursed himself for not explaining more sensibly why he didn't want her to join him. She had opened herself up to him, but he hadn't done the same to her. Not when she'd needed him to.

At the time, telling her as little as possible had made sense. She'd already had an emotionally charged few days with him and had been reserved and withdrawn before the fundraiser. From what he knew of her life, she had good reason not to trust people, and that was why he'd wanted to keep her safe, protect her. That didn't involve exposing her to his fucked-up family or leaning on her emotionally.

What could I have said?

Sure, come back to New York with me, Cassie, but there are a few things you should know. Just off the top of my head: Don't ever be alone with my mother or she will tear you to shreds. Don't ask questions because regardless of who answers, it's probably a lie. Why am I going back? To help a mother despite the fact I'm almost convinced she deserves whatever is happening to her.

I don't sound like a good son, do I?

That's okay. I'm failing at being a good brother and doctor, too.

I took an oath to do everything I could to save lives.

I'm not supposed to hope my mother passes away before I get to her.

In the dark of his room, Luke took out his phone and checked his messages. He had several, but not the one he'd been waiting for. He'd called Cassie soon after he'd left her house, but she hadn't picked up. He'd texted her, but she wasn't responding.

Luke had grown up with power and privilege. Some things came easily to an Andrade, especially in New York social circles. People tended to do whatever he asked. Outside of his family, he couldn't remember the last person who had raised their voice to him. That kind of power was addictive. It could change a person. Luke had watched it allow his family to control people as though they were pawns in some higher game. He'd always held himself above that. At least, he'd told himself he had.

It was tempting to try to win Cassie over with an expensive gesture. He could have pressured her to relent when she'd told him to leave her home. But he believed she would never truly be his unless she came to him.

Cassie closed parts of herself off when she felt threatened. It was what had allowed her to sleep with him even though she was sure he wouldn't stick around. Her need to hold part of herself back had even been evident in their lovemaking, at least until their last time together. For just a short time, she had let him in.

Then her walls had flown right back up at the first hint that her fears about him leaving were justified. He'd tried to keep her from retreating, even physically, and the spark of real fear he'd seen in her eyes had just about broken his heart. It was tangible evidence of what she had endured at the hands of others, and he would never forget that glimpse into the depth of her soul.

It was why he'd given her space when she'd asked for it.

Why he'd left when she'd demanded it.

But, even if she had told him to, he knew he couldn't stop loving her. He'd go to the hospital in a few hours, determine to the best of his ability what was wrong with his mother, set her on a course of treatments if any were appropriate, and then nothing would stop him from returning to Defiance.

And Cassie.

He would win back her trust no matter how long it took.

They belonged together.

Somewhere along the way, Cassie had become a part of him.

THE NEXT MORNING Cassie burned two trays of cinnamon rolls. The batch she didn't burn looked as if a knife-wielding sugar monster had massacred it. She couldn't help it; every time her mind drifted, it returned to what she'd said to Luke the night before and the cinnamon rolls had paid the price.

I am such an idiot. A man tells me his mother is sick, he has to go to her, and what do I do? I think about myself. How this affects me. How scared I am.

Not only do I not ask him if he's okay, or what I can do to help, but I kick him out of my house. Is it any wonder he didn't want me to go back with him?

She thought back to the look of horror in his eyes when she'd told him to take his hands off her. She didn't believe for a second Luke would ever hurt her, but that hadn't stopped her from succumbing to an old panic.

Maybe it's for the best I'm not pregnant. Am I fooling myself when I believe I can change? That I can be stronger?

That the past doesn't have to rule me anymore?

"That one is dead so you can stop frosting it," Tilly said, as she closed the outside door behind her and took stock of Cassie and her kitchen.

Cassie looked down at the mutilated rolls on the tray in front of her and shoved it away harder than she intended. It flew down the counter and landed on the floor in front of Tilly.

Cassie would have normally rushed over, picked it up, and apologized. She didn't. She stayed exactly where she was, staring at it as if it were more damning evidence against her.

Tilly walked around it and went to stand directly in front of Cassie. "Do you have any whiskey?" she asked.

Cassie looked up in confusion. "I don't drink."

"Not for you, for me," Tilly said and opened a cabinet

where Cassie kept alcohol she'd received as gifts from her guests. "Oh, here it is, thank God." Tilly poured herself a shot and downed it.

"I don't think alcohol is good for someone your . . ." Cassie stopped herself and started over. "Are you sure you want to be doing shots this early in the day?" Tilly's son already thought Cassie was a bad influence, Cassie could only imagine what Jimmy would think when she returned home soused by early afternoon.

Tilly poured herself a cup of coffee and sat down with it at the table. "Child, if you could see your face you'd be drinking, too. I have a feeling the story you're about to tell me is going to be a doozy. That shot was to keep these old nerves calm—medicinal purposes. Don't tell my son."

Cassie didn't know if she was about to laugh or cry. She took a few calming breaths.

Tilly raised her coffee cup and referenced the mess around Cassie. "I take it Lover Boy left?"

Cassie picked a roll off the floor and dropped it in the wastebasket. "Yes."

"So, this is your plan to get him back? How's it working out so far?"

To occupy her hands, Cassie began pulling out the burned cinnamon rolls from the trays and throwing them in the trash. "I'd rather not talk about it."

"Of course you wouldn't. Who would want to brag about how they ran a man like that off?"

When she'd finished she turned back to Tilly angrily. "I didn't run him off."

Tilly sipped her coffee without saying a word.

Cassie moved to sit across from her at the table. "I totally ran him off."

Tilly gave her hand a sympathetic pat. "I know you did, Cassie. It's all those hormones they've got you on."

Cassie froze. "Those what?" Bonnie wouldn't have said anything, would she?

"Those fertility hormones. Did you think I didn't know? Cassie, I may be old, but that just means I've seen more than you have. When you first started going to Toledo I thought you had cancer or something. Then you came home with prenatal vitamins, and baby clothes catalogs started arriving. You've made it no secret you want a family, and since there hasn't been a man in your bed outside of our doctor friend, it wasn't a crazy leap."

"You never said anything."

"It wasn't anyone's business but yours. And that's what I told Lenny's mother when she told me her son told her you were just about buying out the pharmacy's home pregnancy test aisle each month."

Cassie shook her head in shock. "Does everyone know?"

Tilly shrugged. "Enough. Nobody cares, Cassie. In fact, knowing made it a whole lot easier for them to put up with your mood swings. Child, we are all waiting for you to birth something so we can get our old Cassie back."

"I'm not pregnant," Cassie said slowly, still a jumble of emotions when it came to how she felt about it.

Tilly looked on with sympathy. "Well, I'm sorry about that. I know you've been trying for a while."

Cassie clasped her hands on the table and focused on a design on the wall behind Tilly. "It's probably for the best. Maybe some people aren't meant to have children."

Tilly slapped her hand down on the table loudly. "You stop yourself right there. I won't sit here while you wallow in pity and put yourself down. I can't stomach listening to people do that to themselves."

Cassie sat up straight. "No one said you had to stay."

Tilly waved a finger at Cassie. "You're going to throw me out? Throw everyone out? That'll make you happier."

"Why should I want you to stay when you just said you don't care how I feel?"

"You, Cassie, need to start listening to people better. I didn't say I don't care. Stop being such a mamby pamby."

"I don't even know what that means," Cassie said angrily and stood, "but I think it's better if you go."

Tilly took another sip of her coffee.

Anger left Cassie as quickly as it had come. Once again, she felt her emotions getting the best of her. She sat back down across from Tilly. "I'm sorry, you've been nothing but a good friend to me, and I—"

Tilly rolled up her sleeves and pointed to the bottle on the counter. "I'm going to need another shot of whiskey if you start crying."

She was so serious that Cassie felt a laugh bubble within. "No one would call you warm and fuzzy."

Tilly didn't look the least bit bothered by that observation. "No, but I'm here." She reached out and took one of Cassie's hands in hers again. "Now tell me what happened between you and Lover Boy, and let's see if we can fix it."

Cassie probably wouldn't have admitted to anyone else what she'd done, except possibly to Bonnie, if she'd used her staring trick on her. "He said he had to go back to New York because his mother is in the hospital."

"And?"

"And he didn't want me to go with him, so I got angry and threw him out."

Tilly made a whistling sound as she took the story in. "What we have here is a clear case of one of you being an asshole."

Cassie's eyes rounded, and she held in another laugh. She never quite knew what Tilly would say.

"Either Lover Boy is married or into something immoral and was lying to you, or you just sent a good man packing because his mother is sick. What are you going to do about it?"

"What can I do?"

Tilly studied Cassie's face. "Before I answer that, I want you to tell me something. Be honest."

"Okay."

"Do you love him?"

Cassie sucked in a gulp of air. "I could. That's probably what made me freak when he said he was leaving. I thought we had something special." She looked down at her hand in Tilly's. "I was getting ready to tell him about the artificial insemination treatments."

"Don't do that."

Cassie's eyes flew up to Tilly's. "You don't think he deserves to know?"

Tilly shook her head. "My husband died not knowing about every man I'd been with, and hell, your last one was a turkey baster. It's best to leave some mystery in a relationship."

Cassie wasn't sure she agreed with that, but she was feeling better about everything, and it was because of one little old woman who wouldn't leave even if Cassie told her to. "Tilly, I love you."

Tilly smiled but pulled back her hand. "Don't go getting all sentimental. You still need to figure out what's going on with your man. I say you fly out there and surprise him."

Cassie swayed in her chair. "You mean fly to New York City. Just like that?"

Tilly took another sip of her coffee. "If he's married, you'll know it. He won't have time to come up with a good lie. And if he's not, if his mother is actually sick, then you belong by his side anyway."

"He told me he didn't want me there."

"Which is exactly why I'd go."

"Plus, I have a business to run. I have orders to fill. I can't just leave. Even if I could, I can't afford it."

Tilly stood up, took out her cell phone, and said, "I'll probably regret doing this, but it's better than watching you mope around until Lover Boy does or doesn't come back." She held up a hand and spoke into the phone. "Myron, I'm at Cassie's house. We need your help." She covered the phone. "I hope I don't have to sleep with him for this."

Cassie's mouth fell open and she pointed to the phone,

which had a speaker nowhere near where Tilly had covered. "He can still hear you."

Tilly turned the phone over to inspect it, then shrugged. "Cassie needs to fly to New York City. I have a project for your girlfriends at the Senior Center. Don't think I don't know who you hang out with every weekend. Go round them up and bring them over to Cassie's. We've got baking to do, and tell them to each bring fifty bucks."

Cassie watched Tilly with a mix of fascination and admiration.

"If you get them over here real quick, I may . . . and this is completely relying on how fast you do this and how well they can bake . . . I may give you that kiss you've been asking for."

Cassie didn't know what Myron said to Tilly, but she actually blushed. "I doubt you're even physically capable of that anymore, Myron, but if Cassie comes home with her man we'll reopen the topic." She hung up on him and grinned. "Men."

Cassie walked over and gave Tilly the longest, tightest hug she'd ever given anyone. Tilly didn't seem to mind one bit.

Chapter Thirteen

CASSIE HITCHED HER purse higher on her shoulder and glanced again at the long security line. She looked back at Bonnie who had insisted on driving her to the airport. "Well, here goes nothing."

Bonnie held up a hand. "You have the address to the hotel in case you need it?"

Cassie patted the pocket of her jacket. "Right here."

"Your cell phone? Cash for the cab? Although I read you can use credit cards, too, but don't flash those around."

"I'll be fine, Bonnie. I grew up in a big city."

Bonnie nodded. "I think I'm more nervous than you are. Someone should be going with you."

Cassie hugged Bonnie tightly. "Everyone has already done more than I know how to thank them for. You. Tilly. Myron. He sure is popular with the ladies, isn't he? There were six ladies working in my kitchen when I left."

Bonnie smiled. "People always want what they can't have, and Myron only has eyes for Tilly. He's been that way as long as I can remember."

Cassie checked the time on her phone. "I need to get in

there."

"Text me as soon as you land."

"I will."

Bonnie bounced with excitement. "This feels just like the part of a romantic comedy where the heroine goes after the hero, and they run into each other's arms as the credits roll."

"He may not want me there, Bonnie. Just because the Turners said he's not married doesn't mean he's not in a serious relationship."

Bonnie pursed her lips briefly. "That's why you have the hotel room. But don't think like that."

Cassie closed her eyes for a moment. It was hard not to. Going to New York was a huge leap of faith, and Cassie didn't make those easily.

As if she knew what Cassie was thinking, Bonnie said, "You took a chance on Defiance, and that worked out for you. Now, defy the status quo and go get your man."

Cassie nodded with determination. With one final hug, Cassie headed into the security line. She walked to her gate with her head held high and took her seat on her plane with resolve. With Bonnie and Tilly's help, Cassie had planned each part of her trip. She had a hotel room to check into upon her arrival. Once there, she would contact Luke. Depending on his response to her unexpected arrival, she would either be staying at the hotel longer, staying with Luke, or flying back to Defiance in the morning.

Tilly and Myron's ladies were running her bed and breakfast in her absence. Between her credit cards and the money she'd tried to refuse but eventually accepted, she could afford to stay in New York for one week. That was plenty of time to figure out if she'd made the right choice by following him.

Cassie had been tempted to tell him she was coming. He'd texted her several times, but both Tilly and Bonnie thought the element of surprise was needed if she wanted his true reaction. Tilly had given her a list of things to watch for as indicators that she should come home. If Luke wouldn't introduce her to his friends or family, it was probably because he didn't want them to know he was cheating. If he didn't want to take her anywhere, that would be another bad sign. Luke had taken her to meet Noah and JoAnne. That had to mean something, didn't it? Neither Tilly nor Bonnie thought Luke was the type to lie, but they admitted he was a man, and no one in the town knew him well.

"Keep your heart open, but be smart," was Tilly's advice.

NOTHING ABOUT THE day had gone well. With his mother still unable to speak for herself and her lawyer battling it out with Gio's, the hospital was scrambling to not only follow the letter of the law but also to appease their largest donors—the Andrades.

Although some of his mother's health issues were heart related, others were arising with no traceable cause. His mother's nurse had described reoccurring low blood pressure, dehydration, and seizures. She'd told the EMT she had grown more concerned when blood had become visible in Patrice's urine. She stated in her admittance paperwork that

Patrice's physician had told her it was a side effect of her medication. According to the EMT, his mother's nurse was young. The nurse had begun to lose faith in the competence of the attending doctor when Patrice's health continued to decline.

Luke could understand why.

Dr. Duce had sent over his mother's medical records, but they were in such disarray Luke couldn't imagine allowing another doctor access to them. Notes were half-written. Pages were missing. Test results lacked dates, names of facilities, or both. It was no wonder Dr. Duce was proving difficult to locate. In Luke's entire career, he'd never encountered such incompetence. Sorting through the paperwork was time-consuming and more than a little frustrating when time was one thing they didn't have a lot of. Patrice's health continued to deteriorate. Her kidneys and liver were close to shutting down. Luke conferenced with the best doctors in every field connected to her symptoms. Everyone required more testing. They were treating Patrice's symptoms as they arose, but Luke was beginning to fear they wouldn't get their answers in time.

Luke returned to his mother's private hospital room and looked down at the frail woman before him, fighting for her life. He regretted every bad thought he'd had about her. She hadn't been the perfect mother, but she hadn't always been the bitter woman she'd become, either.

"How is she?" Gio asked from beside him.

"Worse. If she continues as she is, she won't make it through the weekend."

Luke felt Gio's hand on his shoulder. "I'm glad you're here, Luke."

Luke shook his head in self-disgust. "Why? I haven't figured out what's wrong with her."

With a sad sigh, Gio said, "Even if you don't, you're here, and you're doing everything you can. If she doesn't make it, you'll be able to look yourself in the mirror and know you did everything you could. I'm not sure you could have done that if you'd stayed in Ohio."

"You're right."

"Did you locate her doctor?"

"Not yet. No one has seen him. Mother's records were delivered by a courier."

"Do you find that strange?"

"Extremely." Luke's head snapped around as he sought Gio's eyes. "Why?"

Gio raised and dropped one shoulder. "Maddy said something to me a week ago that I haven't been able to get out of my head."

Luke rolled his eyes skyward. "Maddy."

Gio made a self-deprecating sound. "I know. Usually I don't put much stock in what she says, but there's something you need to know." He let out a long sigh. "I've been working with Dominic Corisi's security specialists, and I believe Mother was behind both instances of money being siphoned out of Cogent. Every ugly paper trail leads back to her. She had someone inside Cogent on her payroll. He's hiding in Argentina now."

"I can't believe she needed the money."

"She didn't. Not for herself. She funneled it to everyone from politicians to CEOs. And she was careful. If we didn't know what to look for, it's possible no one would have ever discovered what she did."

It was too much for Luke to absorb while his mother lay before them unconscious. "I'm sorry, but what you're describing is hard to swallow. She wasn't into politics. What possible reason would she have for bribing politicians?"

Gio shook his head sadly. "I don't know. And we may never know. Part of me wants you to wake her up so we can find out. Then I ask myself: why would she be honest now when she's spent a lifetime lying to us?"

Luke brought the conversation full circle. He didn't want to talk about his mother's indiscretions further, but he was curious about something. "How is any of that connected to her present condition?"

"Maddy warned we shouldn't trust Mother's doctor."

"I'll give her that. He was negligent to the point that I'll be reporting him to the hospital review board. He'll be lucky to keep his license once they investigate his incompetence. I think he deliberately exaggerated her illness at first then covered it up as she actually became ill."

"And . . . why would anyone do that?" Gio asked slowly.

Luke didn't like the expression in Gio's eyes. "What are you suggesting?"

"I'm suggesting you test for everything, even things you wouldn't normally consider."

"Such as?"

He knew the answer even before his brother voiced the word. "Poison."

Chapter Fourteen

CASSIE PACED THE modest hotel room she'd rented. Her luggage was still packed and by the closet. She didn't allow herself to think beyond the steps of her plan.

Get to New York.

Contact Luke.

Deal with whatever she discovered.

She took out her phone and read over the messages he'd sent that she hadn't yet responded to. Four in all. None of them impatient with her. The first apologized for pressuring her. The second said he wished he didn't have to go. The third said he'd be back soon. The fourth said he missed her.

Cassie closed her eyes and clutched the phone to her chest. Luke was a good man. A patient and kind man. When she searched her heart for any real doubt about his integrity, she found none. Although she'd followed Tilly's advice and arrived in New York unannounced, Cassie regretted that decision. Luke didn't deserve to be surprised like that. He had never given her a single reason to believe he would lie to her. She should have called him, told him his absence was unbearable, and offered to come to him.

Should have. Could have. But I didn't. I'm here now.

She sat on the corner of her bed and dialed Luke's number. When he didn't answer, she left what she considered the world's most awkward request for him to call her when he got her message.

Restless, Cassie began to pace her room again. One hour stretched into two. Unable to take it anymore, Cassie left her room and went down to the lobby of the hotel. She sat in the lounge, sipped on water with lemon, snacked on a pretzel and cheese appetizer plate, and tried to distract herself by reading a novel on her phone. She was, however, too distracted to enjoy the story. Each time someone walked into the lounge, Cassie looked up as if it might be Luke—which didn't make sense since she hadn't told him she was there—then, disappointed again and again, she returned to reading even though she couldn't remember the plot of the story.

Still, it was better than sitting alone in her hotel room.

Maybe.

The lounge was mostly empty, outside of a man and woman who were seated at separate tables and were both actively working on their laptops.

A clean-cut man in a business suit, handsome by most standards, walked in and approached Cassie's table. "May I join you?"

Cassie shook her head.

He didn't walk away. "Are you in town for business?" He leaned closer as he asked the question, and Cassie could smell alcohol on his breath.

She looked away, hoping the physical dismissal was

enough. It often was.

This particular man, however, was persistent. He put his hand on Cassie's forearm. Whether it was to get her attention or to slow her if she decided to bolt, Cassie's response was the same. She stood, bringing herself to her full height, and looked him directly in the eye. "If you don't get your fucking hand off me, I will send you to the floor with whatever means I have to. Ever been stabbed with a dull knife? You're about to find out how it feels."

The man raised both hands in the air and his face twisted with disgust as if he'd accidentally bumped into a mentally unstable person. "Hey, take it easy. You were sitting by yourself in a bar. Women do that when they're looking to meet someone."

Cassie glared at him and didn't back down. "I would try to explain to you how obnoxious that sounds, but I doubt it would be worth my effort."

As he looked around the room and realized the two other people in the lounge had stopped working and were watching him, the man's face reddened. He opened his mouth to say something, thought better of it, then walked out of the lounge.

Cassie retook her seat and lifted her glass of water to her lips with a shaky hand. She didn't like when that side of her reared its head. She wanted to be calmer, softer. *Day one in New York and I've already threatened to stab someone. Does someone like me really belong with someone like Luke? You can take the girl out of Detroit . . .*

The sound of clapping surprised Cassie so much she almost dropped her glass. The woman a couple tables over was cheering for her. She stood, tucked her laptop beneath her arm, and walked over to Cassie's table. Her light brown hair was cut in a shoulder-length bob. She was beautifully groomed from head to toe and exactly the kind of person Cassie would have thought her outburst would offend. "Do you mind if I join you?"

Shocked, Cassie merely shook her head.

The woman settled into a seat across from Cassie and held out her hand in greeting. "My name is Jacinda Pickett."

Cassie shook her hand. "Cassandra Daiver. My friends call me Cassie."

The woman smiled. "Wow, that was amazing. I come to the city several times a year for my job, but I prefer the suburbs. My husband says he worries about me, because I'm not tough enough. I don't know what I would have done if that guy had grabbed my arm."

Cassie swirled the lemon around in her glass with a straw and said dryly, "You probably wouldn't have threatened to stab him." The pale blue eyes across from her held no judgment, but Cassie judged herself.

Jacinda shrugged. "No, but I'm going to remember that line. It was really effective."

Cassie looked down before meeting the woman's eyes again. "Thank you."

Jacinda studied Cassie for a long moment. "Do you want to be alone? I didn't mean to intrude."

"No," Cassie said quickly. Jacinda was the perfect distraction. "It's nice to have someone to talk to."

"Are you on vacation or here for work?"

She was usually extremely protective of her privacy, but she doubted she'd ever see Jacinda again and talking about why she was there eased her growing inner panic. "I'm surprising my boyfriend with a visit. Well, I don't know if he's actually my boyfriend. We were together while he was on vacation. He came back to New York for family business, and I missed him . . . so here I am."

"Seriously?" Jacinda asked, then whistled. "I officially now have a girl crush on you. You have guts."

Cassie looked down humbly. "Not usually. But this guy is worth it."

"That is so romantic," Jacinda said with a deep sigh.

Encouraged by her comment, Cassie shared more. "I've never felt like this about anyone. He's sweet but also sexy and strong. He listens to me, but he also knows what he wants. Perfect. I'm the one with the issues. We didn't part on the best of terms, and I regret that."

Jacinda looked toward the lounge entrance. "It'll work out. Imagine if he charged in here and carried you out."

Cassie held up her phone and pressed her lips together. "Not likely since he doesn't know I'm here. And right now he's not answering my call."

"Oh," the woman said sadly.

The lone man in the lounge closed his laptop. "What did you fight about?" Cassie and Jacinda turned to look at the man in surprise. He was an older gentleman with a friendly, relaxed expression. "My wife will want to know when I tell her this story tonight."

The whole conversation felt unreal. Cassie said, "He said he needed to come back to New York because of something going on with his family. I offered to go with him. When he didn't want that, I thought he was feeding me a line."

"And was he?" Jacinda asked.

"I don't know," Cassie answered slowly and chewed her bottom lip. "I don't believe he would lie to me."

The older gentleman asked, "So, you're here to find out if it's the truth."

"Yes."

"Who is this guy?" Jacinda asked. "Not that I would know him, but what's his name?"

Cassie hesitated then asked herself what the chances were that either of them would recognize his name. "Luke Andrade."

"Did you say Andrade?" Jacinda asked in surprise.

"Yes. You know him?"

Suddenly sympathetic, Jacinda said, "Everyone in New York knows the Andrades. His family is worth billions. Oh, honey."

"Billions?" Cassie asked, her voice rising as her nervousness did.

Jacinda shook her head and continued to look sadly at Cassie. "He and his brothers are New York's most eligible bachelors. Although I hear some of them are engaged now. I don't think he is, though."

Cassie's stomach did a painful summersault. "I hope not," Cassie said. A comforting thought occurred to her. "He may not even be one of those Andrades."

Jacinda opened her laptop and typed in something quickly. She turned her computer around for Cassie to see. It was a picture of Luke with his brothers at a restaurant. "Is this your guy?"

Cassie's mouth went nervously dry. "Yes."

"Then he's the one I was referring to."

Cassie stared at the photo of Luke with his brothers. Billions? A man with that much money wasn't moving to Defiance, Ohio. Thinking of Luke as a successful surgeon with rich friends was bad enough. If he really was insanely wealthy, Cassie didn't believe for a moment she was the type of woman he'd want to settle down with.

Which is why he'd agreed to a short vacation fling.

Of course, he'd dressed it up with talk of having feelings for me and wanting it not to end, but men tend to do that rather than be honest. I knew that going into this.

"It was nice to meet you, but I have to go." Cassie stood, put down cash for her food, and gathered her things.

The lone man reopened his laptop and grimaced. "Do you have a way home if things don't work out?"

"I didn't mean to offend you, but . . ." Jacinda started to say by way of apology, but kept the rest to herself.

Cassie nodded once curtly, then walked away from both of them without looking back. She wished she'd stayed in her hotel room.

✦   ✦   ✦

LUKE DRAGGED HIMSELF into his apartment well past midnight. He was physically and emotionally drained. Even if his mother regained consciousness, he knew he and his brothers would never be the same.

When Gio had suggested broadening the range of the tests they had ordered for their mother, Luke had been certain it was a waste of time. He couldn't wrap his mind around anything so heinous happening to his own family.

He was forced to reassess his stance, however, after covertly taking a sample of his mother's blood into the lab himself and testing it. He'd expected to find nothing.

What he'd found had shaken him to the core.

Ricin. By the presenting symptoms, his mother had ingested it in small doses over a period of months. Slowly. Subtly. Low blood pressure. Seizures. Dehydration. Imminent liver and kidney failure. It all made sense when the cause was discovered. Luke had immediately begun treatments to flush her system of toxins and hydrate her. He poured over medical journals about how to treat victims of ricin poisoning. There was no antidote, but if Patrice didn't suffer a systemic shutdown of organs, she had a chance of survival.

Who would poison his mother? Her doctor had to have been involved. There was no other reason for him to exaggerate her illness at first, then cover it up at the end and escape. No reason besides wanting his crime to be discovered too late.

As soon as his mother was stable, Luke had called Gio with his findings and suspicions.

"Did you tell anyone this?" Gio had demanded.

"Of course not, but we need to take this to the police."

"No. We need to handle this ourselves. I've falsified enough documents that we could lose everything, and I could go to jail if an investigation dug deep enough into Cogent."

"I could lose my medical license and end up in the cell next to you if someone discovers I didn't report a poisoning, but that's not the only reason I'm against doing it your way. It doesn't feel right."

"When it comes to protecting the family, I don't care how it feels."

"Are we protecting the family or ourselves?"

"There is no difference for me. I would do all of this for any one of you. There was no loyalty in the generation before us. No love. No sacrifice. And where did it bring us? We decide the future of our family, and I'll be damned if we're all going to pay for something that woman did."

"I'll do it, but I don't like it."

"You can't tell anyone, Luke, or everything we're about to do will only make the situation worse. No one. If you're right about the doctor, he won't get away with it."

"Gio, people might find out what happened. I'm not the only one working with Mother."

"No one will find out because you are a respected surgeon showing interest in his mother's health. No one would have a reason to question you. They'll believe what you say."

Resentment filled Luke. He didn't want any part of this. "I've never been a good liar."

"Well, this is where you become one. Because the alternative is ugly. What would the press do with this knowledge?

Never mind the police. Can you imagine what this would do to our family? If we're really as important to you as you say we are, this is where you prove it. Don't tell Max or Nick. The less they know, the better it will be for them if this goes badly. It won't though, Luke. We won't let it. You and I are going to fix this."

Coldness spread through Luke. "What are you going to do, Gio?"

"Don't worry about me, worry about Mother. Do you think she'll pull through this?"

Sarcastically, Luke had asked, "Suddenly you're concerned with her health?" He expected Gio to defend himself, state he still loved their mother regardless of how he'd distanced himself from her.

Gio had fallen silent for a moment. "I don't want to have to cover up a murder."

Luke hadn't pushed Gio for more than that. What was left to argue? He didn't want to cover up a murder, either.

Stripping, Luke dropped his clothing on the floor as he walked to his bedroom. Never, even when he'd discovered his father had another family in Venice, had Luke imagined his life would come to this. That he would one day be using his talents and his influence, not to cure cancer, but to prevent a scandal unlike anything his family had weathered before.

Luke stepped beneath the hot spray of the shower and tried to wash away the day. He didn't want to be in New York, battling the newest Andrade drama. A part of him loved his mother, even while he felt a growing coldness in his heart each time he thought of her.

Had she embezzled from their family's company as Gio suggested? Why? And how did heading down that dark path align her with a doctor who wanted her dead?

I used to know the right thing to do. I don't know anything anymore. Gio hid the truth about our father because he said he wanted to protect us. I hated him for that. I didn't want to be kept in the dark.

Oblivious sounds pretty fucking nice right about now. No matter how much I don't want to agree with Gio, there isn't a better way to handle this. The police can't be involved. An investigation won't stop with the doctor and the poison. Questions will be asked. Questions that could land Gio in prison. End my career. Destroy what's left of our family.

Thanks again, Mother.

I would have preferred to tell myself that I love you as I fight to save your life.

I hate that you took even that from me.

With his head pounding from the pressure of questions he didn't have the answers to, Luke stepped out of the shower, wrapped a towel around himself, and headed back into his bedroom. He craved the sanity of Defiance, the loving arms of Cassie.

He needed to keep her out of this, especially if there was any chance the missing doctor had been working with anyone. And if the truth did leak out, things could quickly become legally complicated for everyone involved. Cassie had been through enough in her life. He wouldn't expose her to the ugliness in his.

Thank God she's not here.

Dressed in boxers and lounge pants, Luke flipped on his television and lay across his bed on top of the sheets. He picked up his phone and listened to his messages.

Chapter Fifteen

"HE'LL CALL," BONNIE said over the phone.

Cassie plopped back on her bed. She'd used the time while waiting to hear from him to give herself a manicure, a pedicure, and a shave. She had so much time she'd even shaved areas she'd only trimmed before. "Sometimes you just have to face that you're not a size eight anymore."

"You lost me. I'm talking about Luke."

"I am, too. This feels like when I kept trying to squeeze my ass into a size eight pair of pants. I wasn't a size eight. I was a ten. But I didn't want to admit it to myself. I told myself one pair had always been tight. Another had shrunk in the wash. Eventually I couldn't deny it anymore."

"You think Luke doesn't like you because you're a size ten? I've seen him with you. I don't think he cares."

Cassie rolled onto her side and played with the edge of the pillowcase. "I'm saying he's not going to call me back, Bonnie, and sitting here praying he will isn't going to change that."

"He's going to call. You said he was texting he missed you."

"Well, maybe when I didn't answer those texts he moved on."

"Just like that?"

"Just like that."

"Or, maybe, his mother really is sick, and he's by her side, not checking his phone."

"I really want to believe that's true. Not that I want his mother to be sick. You know what I mean?"

"I do. Hang in there. You'll know soon enough."

Cassie stretched out an arm and picked a card off her bedside table. She rolled onto her back and held it up in front of her. "Remember I told you about Luke's cousin, Maddy? She slipped me her number before she left. I couldn't imagine ever calling it when she did, but now I'm tempted. I don't want to go home without knowing the truth."

Sounding doubtful, Bonnie asked, "You really think she'd tell you if her cousin is seeing someone else?"

Cassie thought back to the conversation she'd had with Maddy. "She has a husband and children."

"What does that prove?"

Cassie threw the card down beside her on the bed. "Nothing, I guess. I'm just going crazy waiting. I want to do something."

"Stalking a billionaire will probably get you arrested."

"I'm not going to stalk him, and stop calling him a billionaire. I feel like I'm going to throw up every time you say that."

"I can see how his financial status would make it seem

like this is less likely to work out."

Cassie groaned and covered her eyes. "You're not helping."

"Sorry."

Cassie's phone beeped with an incoming call. She checked it and almost dropped her phone when she saw who it was. "It's him. It's Luke."

"Well, what are you waiting for? Take the call."

"What if he doesn't want me here?"

"Then he's an idiot, and there are plenty more billionaires in the sea. Well, not billionaires maybe, but men with jobs. Go. Before he hangs up."

Cassie sat up in her bed and switched over. "Hello?"

"I miss you, Cassie." Luke's voice was deep, pleased, and heavenly. Cassie closed her eyes and sank back into her bed, savoring the joy that filled her at the sound of her name on his lips.

"I miss you, too." She let out a shaky breath. "Sorry I didn't answer your texts."

"It doesn't matter, Cupcake."

"Yes, it does. You deserved better than that. I don't trust people easily, and when you said you were leaving, I panicked. Then I didn't know what to say."

"It's okay."

"You kept talking about wanting us to have more than a casual thing. I overreacted when you said you didn't want me to go to New York with you. I shouldn't have told you to leave."

"I needed to get back here anyway."

There was something in Luke's voice, a deep sadness that made Cassie want to reach through the phone and hug him. "How is your mother?"

"She's stable, but she's not in the clear yet. The next twenty-four to forty-eight hours will be pivotal." His voice lowered. "It's not easy being away from you, Cassie, but I'm glad you're not here."

Cassie's hand tightened on her phone. "So, now isn't a good time to tell you I'm in New York City?"

"You're where?" His voice rose with an emotion akin to anger. It was the first time Cassie had heard him sound anything like that.

Is that how a man sounds when he's afraid his regular girl-friend is about to discover how he spends his vacations?

"I flew in this afternoon."

"You shouldn't be here," he said in obvious frustration. "Where are you staying?"

Cassie's breath caught in her throat. He was coming to see her. He might not like surprises, but they'd work it out. "I'm at the City View Hotel."

"I'll send a driver for you in the morning. He'll take you to the airport."

"You want me to leave? Just like that? Without even seeing you?"

He sighed. "What I want and what needs to happen are not at all the same right now."

"What are you afraid of? Are you engaged? Or living with someone?"

"I need you to trust me, Cassie. Once this family situation is resolved I'll come back to Defiance, and I'll explain as much of it to you as I can. But you have to go home in the morning."

She wanted to trust him, but he hadn't actually denied seeing anyone else. "Don't send anyone. I have a ticket I can use. I don't need you. But I still can't believe you don't even want to see me. I'm such a fool."

With a pained sound, Luke said, "You're not a fool, Cassie. I meant everything I said to you in Ohio. It's killing me not to come to you tonight."

"You'll have to excuse me if I don't believe you."

"Cassie—"

"There isn't much more to say, is there?" Cassie bit out and hung up.

LONG AFTER CASSIE had hung up on him, Luke paced his apartment, telling himself he'd done the only thing he could. He needed to keep Cassie safe. And that meant keeping her as far away from his family as he could. Being associated with the Andrades in any way could put Cassie in both physical and legal danger. Yes, she was angry with him. Probably hurt. But all of that was preferable to risking anything happening to her because he involved her in any of this mess. Once his mother was conscious and the threat of exposure was past, Luke would go to Cassie and apologize. He'd tell her as much as he could without endangering his family and do whatever it took to gain her forgiveness.

Still he couldn't forget the questions she'd asked him. He

should have done more to reassure her he wasn't with anyone else. Even though he'd told her he'd wanted to see her, she hadn't believed him. Why should she? She had taken a leap of faith and come to him, a move that revealed how she felt about him even if she wasn't willing to say the words yet.

And what do I do?

I send her packing without an explanation.

Of course she thinks the worst.

He tried to get her out of his head.

Told himself to stay away from her.

None of his rational arguments, however, could stop him from getting dressed and driving over to her hotel. He needed to see her. Somehow he had to make her understand she couldn't stay, but that didn't lessen how he felt about her. From the lobby of her hotel, he called her. "I'm downstairs. What room are you in?"

She let out a shaky breath. "Why are you here, Luke?"

Luke didn't know how to begin to explain the ache inside him. His family, their lies: they were huge obstacles standing between him and what he wanted. He wanted to shed them, even if it was only for one night. "Let me hold you tonight, Cassie."

There was a long pause, long enough Luke thought she might have hung up on him again, but then she said one thing—her room number—before hanging up. Adrenaline rushed through Luke's veins, and he strode to the elevators with barely restrained urgency. He didn't want to give himself time to think about all the reasons he shouldn't be there.

She answered the door in an oversized T-shirt and shorts. In one hand she held a stack of tissues. She tossed them behind the door when she realized she was still holding them. Her eyes were puffy and her nose was red from crying, but she'd never looked more beautiful to him.

He stepped inside, slammed the door behind him, and pulled her into his arms. Their kiss was deep and hungry. Luke forgot what he'd wanted to say and gave himself over to the pleasure of her skin, the light scent of her, the way her tongue eagerly met and danced with his.

She broke off their kiss and searched his face. "I want to believe in you."

"You can." There was so much he wanted to say, but so little he could.

"Can I?" She pulled away from him and crossed the room. "Because what you say to me and how you act don't match lately. Any woman would ask herself why." She marched back to stand in front of him and faced him angrily. "Swear to me that you don't have another woman in your life."

"I swear." *I wish it were as simple as another woman.* He didn't say that, though. Instead he pulled her back into his arms. "There is no one else in my life. No one else in my heart. All you have to do is look at me, Cupcake, and I tangle up inside."

She pounded a closed fist on his chest. "Then why send me away?"

He hugged her to his chest and rested his chin on top of her head. "Things are complicated right now. My family is going through a critical time, and they need me."

She relaxed somewhat. "Because your mother is sick?"

"Yes."

"I could stay and support you through this. You wouldn't need to entertain me. I could simply be there for you."

Luke's eyes misted at the sincerity of her offer. Cassie loved, the way a person was supposed to. "You are one amazing woman, Cassie."

"But you still want me to leave? Is it because you don't want your family to know you're with me? I've heard a lot about you since I've been here. They say you're insanely rich. I don't care about that, but maybe you do. Are you embarrassed that I—?" She was speaking softly, sadly.

Her question ripped at his heart. He interrupted her. "Oh, Cassie. No. That's not it." He held her back from him and looked down into her teary eyes. "When my family does meet you, they will love you—just as I do."

Cassie blinked back angry tears. "Don't say you love me then send me away. Don't play me that way."

"This isn't a game, Cassie. I wish I could tell you what's going on, but all I can do is ask you to trust me."

Cassie stood there, glaring at Luke, with her fists clenched at her sides. "I kept a secret from you back in Defiance, Luke. At first I didn't think you would stay, so I told myself it wouldn't matter. Then I was afraid if you knew, you would leave me."

Luke tensed. "What kind of secret?"

Cassie looked down at his hands on her upper arms. "It's

scary, isn't it? Not knowing."

Luke loosened his grip on her, but demanded, "Just say it, Cassie."

She searched his face for a long moment. "I've never had a family. Not a real one. Not the kind you see on television where people argue over chores and everyone gathers for dinner. I want a family, Luke. I want it so much that when I met you I had already started the process on my own. I've gone through three IUI cycles."

"Are you—?"

"Pregnant?" Cassie's lips pressed together sadly. "No. I found out I wasn't right before you left."

"That's why you were so quiet that day." Cassie's secret once again highlighted the difference in how she and Luke had grown up. His heart soared at her disclosure. She had so much love to give. Her children would never know the cold manipulation he and his brothers had grown up with.

"Yes. Having a baby was all I wanted until I met you. Then I started to believe I could have it all. You. A family. That's why I'm here. I wanted more than I had in Detroit, and I made a better life for myself, but I had to fight for it. It wasn't easy, but it was worth it. I want to be with you, Luke, and I'm not afraid to fight for you—for us. If there is anything to fight for. But I can't go back to Ohio and wait for you to come to me. I'm strong, but I'm not that strong. I've been left too many times, and I can't open myself to that kind of hurt again."

Never in his life had Luke seen such honest emotion, and it humbled him. "I can't tell you what's going on, Cassie. It involves more than just me. But I can tell you that you'd be putting yourself at risk if you stayed."

Cassie's chin rose. "You wouldn't let anything happen to me."

She was more right than she knew. His grip on her tightened. "People dream of having money, but what they don't realize is there is always a price to pay. Sometimes it comes for your very soul."

Cassie laid a hand on Luke's cheek. "People without money are tested the same way, Luke. We all get backed into a corner and discover parts of ourselves we don't like, but we can't let that define us. Whatever is going on, Luke, don't let it change you. Don't let it win."

Luke swung her up in his arms and carried her to the hotel bed. Her words had moved him, and he wanted her more because of it. Cassie was as beautiful on the inside as she was on the outside. He wanted to lose himself in her beauty, her goodness.

He needed to.

And he hoped when he woke in her arms the next morning, he would be a man who deserved to be there.

Chapter Sixteen

CASSIE SAT NAKED and cross-legged on the bed munching on bacon and feeding fruit to Luke, who was lying on his side a foot away from her. She caught a glimpse of herself in the mirror and gasped. Her hair was a wild tangle. She tried to flatten one particularly wild curl. "You could have told me I look like I've been pulled through the bushes backward."

Luke shot her his charming, roguish smile that never failed to set her heart beating a mile a minute. "I haven't looked above your shoulders much."

Cassie laughed and threw what was left of her bacon strip at his head. "That's charming."

"It's your fault," he said playfully. "If you weren't so comfortable being naked, I wouldn't be so distracted." He leaned forward, cupping her bare sex with his hand. "Did you shave for me?" He slid a finger between her lower lips slowly, leisurely as if it were his and he had all the time in the world to explore it. When his finger found and began to rub back and forth over her clit, Cassie flushed with excitement.

"My boyfriend likes it."

"Does he?" Luke growled, dipping his middle finger deeper into her while continuing his outer caress. "What else does he like?"

Cassie sucked one of her fingers then trailed it around one of her nipples. She felt herself pucker beneath her own touch. She whispered, "He likes it when I touch myself."

Luke's eyes darkened with passion, and he pushed the tray of food off the bed. It crashed to the floor, but he never took his eyes off Cassie. "I bet he would love to watch you make yourself come. Have you ever done that for him, Cassie?"

Cassie shook her head, already so excited by their game she was breathing raggedly. She slid her hand down her stomach and placed her hand where his had been. She knew her own body, knew how to bring herself pleasure, but she'd never done it while anyone watched her.

She started softly, circling her clit with her finger while massaging one of her breasts with her other hand. All the while, she held Luke's eyes. He took his shaft into his hand and pumped up and down. He was rock hard and so big. Cassie imagined that her finger was the tip of his cock. She pinched one of her nipples and imagined the slight pain was from his teeth.

With Luke, Cassie never felt self-conscious. He was open with his enjoyment of her, and it was impossible to feel anything but sexy when he looked at her the way he did.

Cassie increased the tempo of her fingers on herself and rolled onto her back. Her legs were still crisscrossed, which left her wide open and exposed before him as she began to pump her finger in and out of herself. She rubbed faster, harder, sending herself upward toward a climax. Luke moved closer to her and claimed her mouth with his.

When Cassie cried out in pleasure it was into Luke's mouth. He shifted so he was lying fully against her side and took her hand off herself and brought it to his mouth. He licked each finger as though it were an addictive taste.

"Was it good, Cupcake?" he asked.

"Oh, yes," Cassie said breathlessly.

He kissed his way down her chest, moving down the bed until he was resting between her legs. "Let's compare, shall we?"

There was no comparison. She was already swollen and eager for his touch. His tongue darted across her shaven mound, almost giving her what she wanted, before sliding away. He kissed her inner thighs. Her stomach. He blew softly on her.

Cassie shivered with pleasure. He ran his hands lovingly over her, warming her skin with hot kisses that followed. When Cassie could take no more, she dug her hands into his hair and bucked toward his mouth.

His chuckle was the sexiest sound she'd ever heard, and she knew he was deliberately driving her out of control. By the time his tongue darted intimately into her, she was hungering for it. His unrelenting adoration was an intense pleasure; it was torture. Torture she begged him not to stop. When she was on the brink of another climax, he paused.

She nearly sobbed in disappointment until she heard him opening a condom wrapper. A moment later he went up onto his knees, lifted her hips to his waist, and plunged deeply into her.

Cassie dug her hands into the bed sheets as he took her with a fierceness he'd held back in the past. She came with a cry, but he was beyond hearing her. He thrust harder, deeper, wilder until Cassie lost all concept of where they were or anything beyond them. They fluidly changed their position. It was just the two of them, rising above everything else in a kaleidoscope of searing pleasure. She reached up and pulled his mouth back to hers. He rolled with her, not breaking the kiss, but positioning himself so he could thrust even deeper.

There was an affirmation to their passion that Cassie had never experienced before, a feeling that neither would be the same afterward. When he finally came, they fell, sweaty and dazed, into each other's arms.

For a long time they both simply lay there, enjoying the afterglow. Luke removed his condom, tied and tossed it aside, then kissed Cassie's forehead. "I shouldn't have come here, but I don't regret I did."

Cassie raised her head off his shoulder and looked at him. "I shouldn't have let you in, but I feel the same way. Whatever it is you can't tell me, Luke, I want you to know I'm okay with it. We all have our secrets, and yours don't scare me. I know what kind of man you are. That's what matters to me."

Luke looked at her sadly. "My mother is very ill, Cassie. Very ill. I doubt she'll be with us next week."

Cassie gently caressed Luke's tense jaw. "I'm sure you're

doing everything you can."

Luke covered her hand with his. "You need to know that someone did this to her. I found traces of poison in her system. We think it was her doctor, but we're not sure yet. No one at the hospital knows. Her medical records are all a lie—a lie I'm adding to instead of involving the police." He brought her hand to his mouth. "I'm telling you this because if not saying it costs me you, then it's too high a price to pay."

Cassie sat up beside Luke. "Someone poisoned your mother? Are you serious?"

His steady look told her he was. "If you tell anyone, I could lose everything."

Cassie cocked her head to the side and studied him for a long moment. "Why do I get the feeling you almost want me to?" There in his sad eyes she saw the answer. "You do. You hate what you're doing, and you think you deserve to be punished for it." Cassie took his hand in hers and held it on her thigh. "You picked the wrong person to confess to. I'll take your secret with me to the grave."

Luke frowned. "You understand what I'm saying? I'm falsifying medical records to protect my ass, not for some heroic reason. I'm doing it because the only thing people love more than a success story is tearing one down. The scandal, even after we would prove we weren't involved in it, would ruin my family."

"And you hate yourself for doing something illegal." Cassie laced her fingers with his, looking down at them as she spoke. "I understand better than you know. I told you about my mother. And I told you I stole for survival. I didn't tell you how I felt about it. I had to do it to survive. I had to lie to the police about where she was. I had to lie to my friends so I wouldn't be taken away from her. For a long time, it felt like all I did was lie. I told myself I had to. I saw people hurting people, and I looked away because getting involved would have exposed that my mother wasn't around, and I couldn't risk that. When we're young we think right and wrong are like black and white, easy to distinguish. The reality is that so much of what we do lies in a complicated gray area where there is no right. All we can do is choose the wrong we can best live with."

Luke pulled Cassie into his arms and rolled over so he was above her. "You have a frightening ability to understand me."

"As I said, we're not that different."

He ran a hand through her splayed hair. "What would you say if I told you my mother has been so bitter and so cruel to my brothers and me that I'm forcing myself to get her the best treatments? Part of me would be relieved if she passed away before I saw her again. What kind of son does that make me?"

Slow tears began to spill down Cassie's temples. She tried to blink them back, but Luke's question struck a cord deep inside her. "It makes you human, Luke. My own mother is out there somewhere, probably on a drug binge right now. I tried to save her so many times, but each time I did, she would pull me down with her. I don't understand why, I just know she couldn't let me be happy when she wasn't. I had to walk away from her, Luke. I had to let go. And part of me hopes she overdoses. I don't tell anyone that. It's ugly. It's shameful. But if I'm honest with myself, it's because, although I know I can't open my life to her again, I hate feeling guilty all the time. I want it to end. So, tell me, Luke, what kind of daughter does that make me?"

Wiping away Cassie's tears, Luke said softly, "A beautifully strong daughter of an addict."

Cassie touched his mouth gently with the tips of her fingers. "Then you understand how I see you. You're not a bad person, Luke. Because, if you are, then so am I."

A light beep went off across the room. Luke pulled away from Cassie and picked his pager up off the hotel bureau. "It's the hospital. My mother is awake. I have to go."

Cassie sat up and hugged her knees to her chest. "I'll be here if you need me."

Luke looked across the room at her with so much emotion in his eyes, Cassie almost burst into tears again. "If you're coming with me, you need to shower quickly."

"You want me with you?" Cassie scrambled off the bed.

Luke held out his hand to her. "Not in her room. My brothers will want to be alone with her, I'm sure. But we have a private waiting room for family."

Family.

Cassie followed Luke into the bathroom and took a brief shower with him. The sexual tension of earlier was absent as they rushed to dress and gather their things, but one word kept echoing in her head.

Family.

It was difficult to mesh how awful the events of the day were with how wonderful that one word made Cassie feel. Luke called his brothers, informing them to meet him at the hospital. She heard him tell one of them he was bringing her, and she held her breath.

✧ ✧ ✧

LUKE CALLED MAX first and told him to bring Nick to the hospital. He put off calling the more difficult of his brothers until he and Cassie were just about to walk out of her hotel room.

"Gio, the hospital called. Mother is conscious and coherent. I'm heading over there now. Max and Nick are on their way."

Gio made a sound deep in his throat. "I wish you'd give us time to talk to her first. Alone."

"She doesn't have much time, Gio. She's awake, but she's not pulling through as I'd hoped. This could be the last time they see her."

"Shit. You did the right thing then."

Luke met Cassie's eyes and took her hand in his. Right. Wrong. No, this was neither. There was only one right thing in his life, and he was taking her with him to the hospital. "Cassie is coming with me."

"You're taking a big risk, Luke. I wouldn't bring her."

"She's coming, Gio."

Gio swore. "Tell me she doesn't know."

"I trust her."

"You barely know her," Gio thundered. Cassie winced as

Gio's voice reached her.

Luke gave Cassie's hand a firm squeeze and held her gaze. "I trust her more than most people I've known my whole life. She's part of my life, and she deserved the truth. Did you tell Julia?"

"Yes," Gio said quietly. "Julia doesn't want to be protected from the truth, and I respect that."

"Then understand it's the same with Cassie."

Gio sighed. "I hope you didn't just make a monumental mistake."

"I didn't," Luke said firmly. "I'll see you at the hospital."

As he and Cassie rode alone in the elevator, Cassie said, "If my presence will upset your family, I'm okay with not going."

Luke fell in love with her a little bit more just then. "Gio always sounds that way. You'll get used to it. He's worried, and he's used to being in charge. There isn't much about this that's in his control, and that's not easy for him."

"Are you close?"

"I spent my life trying to be. I don't know if it's important anymore. When my mother passes, we may all end up simply going our separate ways." Luke surprised himself with how jaded he'd become. Yes, his brothers seemed to have reconciled, but they'd been in that place a hundred times before only to fall apart again. It was difficult to imagine their fragile bond would withstand the stress that losing a parent put on any family.

Cassie clung to his hand, but she didn't debate his last comment to her. He had a feeling she would support his decision either way. He'd never had that type of love in his life before, and he wanted it there beside him today. Cassie's support was his beacon of light in the dark, bottomless hole he found himself in.

When they arrived at the hospital, Luke introduced Cassie to the three women gathered in the private waiting room beside his mother's room. Gio's fiancée, Julia, hugged him tightly then hugged Cassie just as awkwardly and long. Luke had known Nick's fiancée, Rena, for most of his life. He was glad to see her there to support his brother. Tara, Max's fiancée, was a newcomer to the group and tentatively hugged Luke, expressing her hope that Patrice would recover.

Before walking out of the room, Luke took Cassie aside. "I don't know how long I'll be in there."

Cassie gave him a supportive smile. "I'll be fine."

He opened his mouth to say something else, but Cassie covered his lips with her hand.

"Don't worry about me, Luke. Go be with your brothers. I'll be here when you're done."

Luke kissed her warmly, tenderly, absorbing as much of her goodness as he could before turning away. He spoke briefly to the attending doctor about his mother's condition then read over her latest stats. It didn't look good. Her body was shutting down. He considered calling for a morphine drip, but she was alert, communicative, and didn't appear to be in pain. He would have called it a miracle, but there was nothing holy or likely good about giving his mother one last chance to speak.

Luke's brothers were already gathered around her bed.

Luke headed that way, but Nick met him halfway, shaking his head in disgust. "She doesn't care that any of us are here. She wants to speak to Uncle Victor. Should we call him?"

Chapter Seventeen

"IT'S NICE TO finally meet you," Julia, Gio's fiancée, said as she took a seat in the waiting room beside Cassie. "Gio told me Luke had met someone." She quickly reintroduced the other two women in the room.

Cassie clasped her hands on her lap. "I know it's not good timing, but I'm glad to finally meet all of you. Luke doesn't talk much about his family."

"Really?" Rena asked, her voice rising slightly. "That's surprising. He has called each one of them every few days for as long as I've known them, and that's a long time. Nick didn't know what to do when he didn't hear from him for two weeks."

Julia added, "I consider Luke the glue of his family. Gio was just as lost when he didn't hear from him. It's funny how easy it is to take someone for granted. When Gio said Luke didn't want to come back, I was getting ready to fly out there and beg him to. These Andrade men don't know how to express it well, but they love each other."

Tara nodded in understanding. "Max was exactly the same. He doesn't like to talk about his childhood, but we've

199

been fixing up the houses on Slater Island for all of you. He knows you'll want to decorate them to your own taste, but he is happy when he's there working with contractors on those homes. It's like they are tangible evidence of his bond with his brothers."

Cassie didn't know what they were talking about. "What houses?"

Tara looked at the other three women as if confirming that it was okay to share, then said, "Max bought five homes on Slater Island off the Rhode Island shore. It's kind of a long story, but his uncles had an island back in Italy that was supposed to be passed down to Gio."

Rena leaned toward Cassie. "Then Patrice stepped in."

Julia pursed her lips sadly. "She does like to make her sons suffer, doesn't she? She lied to them about the island. Told her sons the uncles were denying them their inheritance because they didn't consider them worthy of it."

Rena nodded. "Then their uncles sold the island to Dominic Corisi."

Julia blinked a few times as if remembering an event. "Gio was angry, but things became bad between him and his mother when he found out the role his mother had played in losing the island."

Cassie looked from woman to woman. "So, Max bought homes on another island to replace what they'd lost?"

Julia tapped a finger on the armrest of her chair. "Yes and no. Gio owns half of the Italian island now. His cousin, Stephan, owns the other half. I think Max wanted to recreate some of that. What do you think, Tara?"

Feeling overwhelmed, Cassie let out a breathy chuckle. "I am so lost right now. Fascinated, but lost. Why five homes? One for their mother?"

Rena gave Cassie a pat on the arm. "Hell, no. The fifth house is for Gigi."

"Gigi?" Cassie echoed.

Tara's eyes rounded. "Should we be telling her all this?"

Rena nodded. "She's here, so I say yes. Luke doesn't bring women around to meet the family. Ever."

Julia rolled her eyes in agreement. "And getting information out of an Andrade is like pulling teeth."

It was impossible not to want to hear the rest of the story. Cassie prodded, "So, who is Gigi?"

Tara raised a hand at Rena. "I know you've known them longer, but let me try to explain it. You chime in if I'm wrong anywhere."

Rena shrugged and waved to give her permission to continue.

Tara tapped each of her fingers as she spoke as if checking off points. "Their father, George Andrade, never divorced Patrice, but he wasn't happy. He had a secret second family in Venice. Gigi is the daughter of that relationship and therefore their half-sister." Tara smiled proudly. "Right?"

Rena nodded. "That sums it up."

"And Max bought her a house. That is so beautiful."

Tara raised and dropped a shoulder sadly. "It would be, if she knew about it. They keep trying to contact her, but she won't speak to any of them. They didn't know she existed until recently, although she knew about them. Apparently she'd been told not to contact them while Patrice was alive."

Cassie grimaced. "That's horrible."

Rena made a face. "That's Patrice."

Cassie sat back in her chair and added what she'd just heard to what she knew about Luke and his brothers. "So, the houses on Slater Island represent a second chance for them to be a family." Her eyes misted up. "That is so sad and so beautiful."

Julia leaned over and hugged Cassie. "I know this is premature, but I love you already."

Chapter Eighteen

VICTOR ANDRADE WALKED into Patrice Stanfield's hospital room with his shoulders high and a determined set to his jaw. He was in his early sixties, but he still had a powerful presence. His features softened when he saw the tubes and machines attached to his sister-in-law. "I'm here, Patrice."

"Leave us," Patrice said to her sons in a weak voice.

Gio was the first to respond. "Whatever you have to say to Victor, you will say in front of us."

Luke took his place beside Gio, lending him unspoken support. Nick and Max joined him.

Victor stepped closer to the bed. "Patrice, do you want me to call a priest? Whatever you have to say might be better said to God."

Patrice's eyes narrowed. She spoke softly, but there was steel in her voice. "God didn't sleep with me then toss me aside like I was a common whore. You did."

Victor's face whitened. "That was a long time ago, Patrice. We were young. Things happened, but I thought you understood we were never more than friends."

"I loved you," Patrice spat. "But you ripped my heart to shreds and fed it back to me each time I saw you with that Italian slut."

Victor was quiet in the aftermath of her announcement.

Luke, appalled, looked over at Gio. His cheeks were flushed with anger, but that was the only sign he was also shocked by the announcement. Nick on the other hand was barely concealing his revulsion, and Max was looking like he was ready to walk out of the room. None of them moved, however.

Finally, Victor said, "I didn't know, Patrice. When we spoke about it afterward, I thought you understood. Then I met Katrine, and you said you were happy for me."

"Happy? How could I be? She stole the only thing that ever mattered to me."

Victor frowned. "I was never yours, Patrice."

An ugly expression spread across Patrice's face. "I hate you for that. I married George because I wanted you to feel as badly as I did. But you didn't care."

"George loved you," Victor said firmly.

"George was a fool. He knew how I felt about you, and he married me anyway."

The monitor on the wall revealed the toll Patrice's anger was taking on her. Victor looked at the monitor then said, "Try to stay calm. I don't know why you want me here, Patrice. Say what you want about my brother, but he was a good man. Not a perfect one, but a good one. He loved his family very much."

"He proved his love every time he flew off to his Venetian mistress."

Victor shook his head sadly. "He would have given her up for you, Patrice. You know that."

"I didn't want him," Patrice snarled. She looked behind Victor at her sons. "I should never have had children with him. I see you and what you did to me every time I look at them. Gio has your judging eyes. Nick has your Andrade charm. Luke has his father's heart, and it sickens me to watch him grovel for my approval. And Max. He looks just like you, Victor. He should have been ours, but he isn't. And he walks away from me just as easily as you always have."

Luke let out a breath he hadn't realized he was holding in. Part of him wanted to walk away and pretend he'd never heard any of this. However, part of him knew he needed to hear the rest.

Victor was reeling beneath the depth of Patrice's bitterness. He was visibly shaken.

Gio said quietly, "Is that why you made sure Victor lost his company? Because he didn't choose you?"

Victor looked back at Gio. "What are you saying?"

Gio's hands fisted at his sides. "Tell him, Mother. Tell him how you bribed everyone with Cogent's money. To do what? Block enough of his business deals to sink his company? That's what you did, isn't it?"

Patrice brought a shaky hand to her face. "You wouldn't stay away from my family, Victor. When George died, you tried to take the only thing I had left—my sons. I wanted them to hate you the way I do."

Victor's shoulders shook with emotion and his voice was

unsteady as he said, "You hated me that much?"

"Yes," Patrice said. "And I'm glad you know. I beat you, Victor. I wanted to see your face when I told you. Maybe you didn't love me, but in the end, I won."

Tears began to run down Victor's face. He looked down at Patrice then back at his nephews without wiping them away. "You didn't win, Patrice. No one in this room did. I'm sorry I didn't love you. I'm sorry I slept with you that night. I didn't do it to hurt you. Our families were close. I cared about you. I had no idea you felt this way. I don't know what I would have done differently if I had known how you felt. It wouldn't have changed anything with Katrine. But, maybe I could have said something that would have stopped you from going so far."

"You still would have lost your company, Victor. I only helped you along."

"You think I'm talking about a company?" Victor's voice rose with rage. "Look at your sons, Patrice. Look at them. Four healthy, successful men. You should be proud. They love you, although you have done nothing to deserve it. My brother loved you, and you shame his memory. I pray for your soul, Patrice. I pray for your sons, that they realize they deserved better than you gave them."

"Get out," Patrice said, bringing a shaking hand to her chest. "Go home to your wife and try to live with what you've done to me."

Victor stepped away from her bed. "What *you* have done, Patrice. *You* brought this on yourself."

He wiped the tears from his cheeks and met the eyes of

each of his nephews. He said nothing, but there was nothing he could say. He walked out of the room, and Patrice let out an angry, vile cry.

Alarms on the monitors began to go off. An emergency team rushed in. Luke knew they wouldn't win. His mother's obsession had just walked out the door, and her fury with him was more than her heart could handle—literally.

The team asked Luke and his brothers to step out of the room so they could work on her. Together, they walked into the waiting room. Gio opened his arms and Julia ran into them. Nick went to hug Rena. Max walked over and pulled Tara into his arms.

Luke met Cassie's eyes, but didn't walk toward her. He felt raw and exposed. He knew his mother was likely taking her last breaths in the other room, and he didn't have the slightest desire to help the team save her. Although he knew Cassie would say she understood, he couldn't go to her as he was.

He was filled with anger the likes of which he'd never experienced before. Everything his mother had said, everything she'd done, shook Luke. Had she always hated looking at her sons, or had there been a time, at least when they were little, when she'd felt something for them?

He'd told Cassie he loved her, but in that moment he doubted he was qualified to know what love was. Cassie stood and took a step toward him.

Luke turned and walked out of the waiting room.

He knew what he had to do.

✧   ✧   ✧

CASSIE DIDN'T MOVE from her spot in the middle of the room. At first she told herself he would be right back. He probably had to speak to a fellow doctor, or he was returning to his mother's side. That wasn't the look she'd seen on his face, though.

In her heart, she knew he was gone.

The chatter of talk around her filtered through her shock, giving her the reason he might bolt. His mother had had a myocardial infarction and wasn't reviving. *This is not about me. This is not about my fear of being abandoned again. Luke trusted me enough to bring me here. If he needs to be alone to deal with his mother's death, I can't judge him for that.*

A tall, dark-haired man came to stand beside Cassie. He spoke with a heavy French accent. "You must be Cassie. I'm Maddy's husband, Richard."

Cassie spared him a quick glance. "That's me," she said, before looking back at the door.

"He'll be back. Luke is one of the finest men I have met. And the most loyal."

Cassie believed him, but it didn't make Luke's departure easier to endure. An old panic was nipping at her heels, begging to take over her mood. She was fighting it, but was winning only with sheer determination not to succumb to it. "I know."

Richard put a comforting hand on Cassie's shoulder. "Sometimes when a man loves a woman, he tries to protect her from his inner demons. Especially on a day when they are raging, you understand?"

Cassie met the kind eyes of the Frenchman. "I think so."

Pressing his lips together in a sad line, Richard continued, "It is often best to let him. Luke is no coward. His uncle left with tears in his eyes. I don't believe they were from mourning. Whatever Patrice said to him, it was ugly. And if Luke heard her, then it's my guess *that* is what he is running from."

Cassie turned to face Richard. "What would she have said? And how do you know?"

Richard made a pained face. "Patrice has been an unhappy woman for a very long time. I don't want to imagine what she would use her last breaths to say."

Maddy burst into the waiting room and sought the arms of her husband. Tears were running down her face. "She's gone, Richard. I know Uncle Victor wanted to talk to her first, but I should have gone in with him. I should have made him let me. I didn't get to say goodbye."

Richard hugged his wife to his chest in a comforting, almost rocking move. Maddy sobbed softly against him. He reassured her in a gentle tone, "It's okay, ma petite chouchou. She knew you loved her."

Gio walked over to where they were standing and said, "Madison."

Maddy raised her head, her cheeks covered with her tears.

A muscle in Gio's jaw flexed visibly, but when he spoke his voice was as tender as Richard's had been. "My mother went quickly, but she mentioned you."

"She did?" Maddy asked sadly, hopefully.

Gio continued, "She asked me to thank you for being so

good to her. She was sorry she never told you she loved you, but she wanted you to know that she did."

Visibly shaking, Maddy threw herself into Gio's arms and burst into tears again. He hugged her, the look he gave Richard above Maddy's head revealed the truth. Patrice had said no such thing.

Richard's eyes misted with grateful tears when Maddy returned to him a moment later, smiling through her tears. Maddy said, "See, Richard, she did love me. I knew there was good in her."

Cassie looked away, feeling awkward to be inside such an intimate family moment. Her phone rang. *Luke.* "Where are you?" Cassie asked, trying not to sound as desperate as she felt.

"My mother's gone, Cassie. They announced her time of death."

"I know."

"I should be there, right beside you, but I can't be. I need—"

"I understand, Luke."

"Do you? Because I don't. I just know I can't face you like this. A driver is downstairs. He'll take you back to your hotel. I told his service he's to stay with you for as long as you need him. Tomorrow also, if you'd like. So, when you're ready to go to the airport, tell him. Also, he has instructions on how to arrange my plane to take you back. Your hotel is paid up until tomorrow night. If you stay longer, they have instructions to bill me."

"Luke, are you going away because you're worried about

what we talked about earlier?"

He let out a disgusted sigh. "No. The documentation is sufficient so there shouldn't be any issues."

"Then why?"

"I need time, Cassie. I'll call you."

Cassie raised her chin. *He's not my mother. He's not one of the men who have disappointed me. This is Luke, and he's hurting. I can do this.* "I'm not going anywhere, Luke. I'm going to stay right here in New York. I'm not leaving you."

"I don't want to hurt you, Cassie, but I can't think right now. I need to get out of the city. And I need to do it alone. I'm sorry."

"You lost your mother today, Luke. Don't be sorry. Just know I'm here for you when you're ready."

He hung up and Cassie slowly pocketed the phone. She closed her eyes and took a fortifying breath. When she opened them, she realized Gio, Maddy, and Richard were watching her with interest. She forced a brave smile to her lips. "Luke said he needs a little time to clear his head."

Maddy hugged her. "Are you okay, Cassie?"

Cassie nodded. "I'm fine." She walked over to one of the chairs and picked up her coat. "I'm going to go now."

Gio beckoned Julia over. The two of them exchanged a look, then Gio said, "Cassie, Julia and I have a guest bedroom. We want you to stay with us."

Although she appreciated the offer, Cassie couldn't imagine taking them up on it. "Thank you for offering, but I have a hotel room already."

Gio waved for Nick and Max to approach. "I need to

stay here to make arrangements for Mother. One of you needs to escort Cassie back to her hotel to collect her things."

The last thing Cassie wanted was to be alone in her hotel room again, but she also didn't feel right about imposing on Luke's family. They were all reeling from a loss. None of them needed the added responsibility of Luke's ditched girlfriend.

Nick looked at Rena and said, "I say we toss a coin, and the winner takes her."

Rena smacked him on the arm. "I know you joke when you're uncomfortable, but stop because Cassie doesn't know us yet."

Cassie squared her shoulders. "I'll be perfectly fine at my hotel. Really."

Julia put a hand on Cassie's arm. "I have the perfect idea. Why don't I take Cassie back to collect her things? Gio, you finish up at the hospital. Then everyone come over tonight for dinner." When no one agreed, Julia added, "We'll need to make funeral arrangements, contact people. Plus, I think it would be nice to be together tonight, don't you?"

Slowly, they all agreed to meet that evening, and one at a time the couples left.

Julia stayed with Cassie and walked down to the hospital foyer with her. Cassie told Julia once more that, although the offer had been kind, she thought it was best if she stayed at the hotel. Julia helped her locate Luke's driver then climbed into the car beside her.

Cassie's head was still spinning; the day had taken on a surreal feeling. She didn't actually want to be alone, but she also had no idea how to handle Julia.

Julia interrupted her thoughts. "I know what you're thinking. Meeting everyone can be a little overwhelming, but we do want you with us. You seem like the quiet type, though. I should warn you that you have to speak up for yourself, or the Andrades will steamroll right over you. They can be pushy."

"You mean like escorting me back to my hotel to pack me up even after I refused the offer?" Cassie parried gently.

A sheepish grin spread across Julia's face. "Oh, my God. You did say no, didn't you? They must be rubbing off on me."

Cassie shook her head in humor. It was impossible not to like Julia. "You win. I'll go with you peacefully."

Julia's smile shone. "You weren't going to be given much of a choice." She sighed happily. "Gio and I have been trying to plan our wedding, but things keep cropping up. I was starting to worry, but what's a piece of paper? In my heart, I'm already an Andrade. I can't wait to tell Gio. He'll get a kick out of that."

Speaking before she filtered her thoughts, Cassie blurted, "You and Gio seem so different."

Julia smoothed the skirt of her dress. "On the surface we are, but not where it matters. Gio is actually really funny when he lets his guard down. You have to understand, he wasn't raised in a home where people expressed their emotions, and so he has difficulty doing it. Luke's the same. Weakness was manipulated or shamed by their mother. My guess is that's why Luke doesn't want you to see him upset.

He's hurting. Give him time."

"I am," Cassie said simply. *At least, I'm going to try my best to.*

"I was watching Gio's face when you were talking to Luke. Whatever you said really touched Gio. That's why he wants you with us. Family is everything to Gio."

Cassie gasped as Julia's words rocked through her. "I'm not family." *Not yet. Maybe not ever, if Luke doesn't come back to me.*

Julia's expression turned sympathetic. "You will be. Luke wouldn't have brought you to the hospital unless his intentions were serious. I know he told his brothers he loves you." Cassie was still getting over that surprise when Julia added, "When things settle down, you and I should go ring shopping. It's only a matter of time."

Cassie fought to stem the panic rising within her. "Shouldn't I wait to see if he comes back and then if he proposes?"

Julia dismissed her worries with a wave of her hand. "You need to think more positive than that, Cassie. I read motivational books. Life is like driving a car. You end up where you put your focus. Believe he's coming back to you, and he will."

Cassie smiled as a warm feeling spread through her. An image of Emma, the woman from Ohio, flitted through Cassie's mind. She had the strangest feeling Emma was still with her, whispering that family can happen anywhere. In Ohio. Even in New York.

The town car pulled up to the front of Cassie's hotel.

Before getting out, Cassie turned to Julia and, in a voice thick with gratitude, said, "Thank you, Julia."

Julia smiled back warmly. "Thank me later by helping me make dinner. Maddy says you're a wonderful cook."

Cassie froze. "You talked to Maddy about me?"

"Why, did you tell her something you shouldn't have?"

"No," Cassie said quickly.

Julia laughed. "By the horror in your voice, I can tell you've already discovered Maddy is an awful secret keeper. But don't worry; she was surprisingly tight-lipped about you. I'll admit I was curious enough to try to pry information out of her, but all she talked about was what great scones you make."

So, no one besides Maddy believes I may be pregnant with another man's baby.

Thank God.

I'll have to address that misunderstanding the next time I see her.

Especially since I'm staying with Luke's family.

Cassie's breath caught in her throat and her mouth went nervously dry.

I'm staying with Luke's family.

✦   ✦   ✦

THAT EVENING, LUKE made himself a Dewar's and water in the living room of the home Max had given him on Slater Island. The fire he'd made to warm the room reminded him of Cassie and his first night at her bed and breakfast.

Not that he needed reminding. She was entwined within

every thought he'd had since he walked away from her. After ensuring he'd left his mother's medical records in order, falsehoods and all, Luke had started back to the waiting room to meet her then stopped.

He wasn't the same man who'd brought her with him to the hospital. Something inside him had died while listening to his mother attack his uncle. She'd always had a vicious side to her, but what he'd seen in her eyes when she'd looked at Victor had been real hatred, hatred so dark it had ruled her.

He'd always told himself he'd imagined how she'd looked at her children. He'd made excuses for her cutting remarks. Most recently, he'd told himself she might have early signs of dementia.

That wasn't what she presented in her final moments. Viewing his mother as a case study gave Luke the emotional distance to sort through what he'd learned about her during her final moments.

Patrice Stanfield had married a man she didn't love to get back at the man she claimed to. She'd borne four sons to him, sons she couldn't love because they were a constant reminder of the man who didn't return her feelings. In her need to make Victor pay for not loving her, she used her sons as pawns to hurt him, used her connections to ruin his company, and in the end, wasted her final breaths exposing him. No remorse. No regret.

Some would diagnose her a classic sociopath.

Nothing his mother had said to Victor had been designed to hurt her sons. It was quite clear they were not important enough to warrant her vengeance.

Something had snapped inside Luke when he realized how utterly unimportant he and his brothers were to the woman who had raised them. He no longer cared why her doctor had poisoned her. He guessed it had been money related.

So, Luke had ensured no one would ever know about the ricin. Her murder was as unimportant to him as his life had been to her.

If it had even been a murder. His mother's heart attack had occurred during her fit of fury. It was somewhat ironic she might have died that way regardless of the poisoning.

Either way, he felt nothing about her death.

Nothing for his brothers.

Nothing at all.

Which was why he couldn't see Cassie like this. He'd told her he loved her. He'd implied they would spend the rest of their lives together. So, how then, could he feel nothing for her either? She had been through so much; he didn't want to hurt her more. He knew, though, if she looked into his eyes now, she would know the truth.

He was hollow.

Luke spun on his heel at the sound of the front door of the house opening and closing. He walked to the foyer, not wanting it to be, but hoping it would be Cassie.

Uncle Alessandro walked straight toward him. He was in his early sixties like Victor, but often looked younger because of the warm smile that never left his face. He wasn't smiling as he approached Luke. "How are you?"

"Fine," Luke said calmly, dismissively.

Alessandro sniffed audibly. "Been drinking?"

"Not nearly enough," Luke said dryly and took another deep gulp.

"You have your brothers worried."

"They'll get over it."

"You have your uncles equally worried."

Luke slammed his glass down on a table. "I said I'm fine."

"You've had a rough month, Luke. First your friend passed away and now your mother. That would shake any man."

Glaring at his uncle, Luke snapped, "I came here to be alone, Alessandro."

His uncle looked around the large foyer before answering. "Did you? You chose an interesting place to hide. Max told me he bought these homes as a place for your family to start over. What are you looking for here, Luke? Because this is just stone and mortar. Your family is back in New York, and they need you."

"Me? No. When it comes to being a doctor, I'm good. I save lives. But with family? Nothing I do makes a damn bit of difference. If you're so worried about my brothers, go be with them."

Alessandro straightened his shoulders and advanced on Luke. "And leave you here, drowning your sorrows in alcohol? No. You're coming back to New York with me."

Luke's temper began to rise. "I don't want to have to throw you out of my house, Alessandro."

"Try to," Alessandro said, and slammed one of Luke's shoulders. Luke was as stunned as he was infuriated by the action. He'd never seen this side of his uncle before.

"Get out."

"Make me." Alessandro pushed Luke back another step.

Planting his feet and clenching his hands at his sides, Luke snarled, "Don't touch me again."

Alessandro went nose to nose with Luke. "Or what? What will you do?"

"Get out of my house," Luke roared, angrier than he could put in words.

"Good," Alessandro said, stepping back. "Get angry. You should be angry. Victor told me what happened at the hospital."

Luke picked up the glass beside him and threw it furiously across the room. It shattered against the wall and fell to the floor. It was the first time in his life he'd lost control like that, and it felt strangely good.

Alessandro nodded in approval. "Yell. Scream. Break every damn thing in this house. It needs to come out."

Luke ran his hands angrily through his hair and growled. "I hate her, and I hate who I am because of her."

In a gentle tone, Alessandro asked, "Who are you?"

Slamming a hand down on the table beside him, Luke yelled, "I thought I knew. I thought I had all the answers. Now I don't know anything. Not one fucking thing. I love my profession, but I don't ever want to step foot in that hospital again. I thought I was a good brother, so why am I here and not with them? And why, if I'm in love with Cassie, do I not want to be with her?"

"Is that a fire I hear in the other room? Let's go sit down, Luke. I want to tell you a story."

Luke took a calming breath and followed his uncle into the living room. They sat across from each other on chairs in front of the fireplace. Luke sat with his head in his hands. Still angry. Still confused.

"Your mother wasn't always bitter and obsessed with Victor. Her family met ours while vacationing in Italy when I was in my early teens. Patrice was a beautiful girl from an insanely rich family who gave her everything. I don't think Patrice had ever wanted something and been denied it until she decided she wanted Victor. At first it was cute. She had a crush on him. As we grew older, she hid her feelings better, but they were still obvious to anyone who knew her. Victor liked her, but not in the way she wanted him to. They foolishly explored that connection. Victor didn't tell me what happened, but I knew. Your father knew, too. Patrice was openly desperate to gain Victor's attention. But Victor met Katrine right after that, and there was no other woman for him. I felt for Patrice. She was deeply hurt. George felt the same, and more. He'd always loved Patrice. One of the happiest days of his life was when she married him."

Luke rubbed his hands over his face. "You're not telling me anything I don't know. My mother was clear about how and why she did what she did."

Alessandro rubbed a hand across his forearm and looked into the fire. "You know the facts, but I want to make sure you understand your mother was genuinely hurt by Victor's disinterest in her. Now, people get hurt every day. Many endure much worse than a broken heart and heal. Your mother held her anger inside her and let it fester there until she was nothing more than a woman who had been wronged. You're angry, Luke. And you have a right to be. What are you going to do with that anger? Will you grow from it? Become a better person because of it? Or will you be a casualty of it?"

Luke closed his eyes and admitted, "I wanted to save her."

Alessandro cleared his throat. "With age comes, if not wisdom, then at least more experience. You do have your father's heart, Luke. But it doesn't make you weak." Luke opened his eyes and met Alessandro's, which shone with emotion. "George was a good man. A better man than I'll ever be. He loved people with everything he had in him. He was the one who first said, 'I'm an Andrade, and to an Andrade, family is everything.' The best parts of Victor and me are because George set an example for us. An ideal. I used to tease him about how sentimental he could be, but he had it right. Victor and I were extremely competitive when we were younger. Victor's the youngest, but he should have been born first. He has always seen himself as the head of our family. When we were young, we fought because of that. When George died, I decided to let Victor play the role that makes him happiest. Even at my home, he likes to be the one who gives the dinner toasts. What once made me angry now amuses me. They say that family is a gift, but it's also a choice, Luke. Not always an easy one, but the only one that matters in the end."

"Your story would be much more touching if my father hadn't had a second family in Venice," Luke said.

Alessandro shrugged one large shoulder. "Your father was human, but he loved you. I miss him every day. You still have your three brothers, Luke. They're not perfect, but treasure them while they are with you. None of you will be here forever."

Luke stared into the fire, losing himself in the flames as he thought about his brothers. He couldn't imagine how he'd feel if he were to lose one of them.

"Gio may drive you crazy, but he and Julia welcomed your lady friend into their home."

Luke looked at Alessandro in surprise. "They did what?"

"I hear Cassie is staying with them until you return for her."

Luke frowned. "I thought she was going back to Ohio."

Alessandro shrugged again. "Women. They do as they please."

"Did you see her? How is she?"

"This Cassie. Do you think she is the one for you?"

"I thought so."

Alessandro stood. "Don't confuse how you feel today with what is in your heart. Get some rest tonight, Luke. Your head will be clearer in the morning. But either way, be honest with her, and don't make her wait too long. She deserves that much, no?"

"Yes."

Luke walked Alessandro to the door, and they hugged

briefly before Alessandro left. *Yes, Cassie deserves the truth.*

And I'll tell her how I feel—as soon as I figure it out for myself.

Chapter Nineteen

A WEEK LATER, Cassie put her luggage down just inside the door of her kitchen and didn't know if she should laugh or cry when she saw Tilly sitting at the kitchen table waiting for her. The trip home hadn't been an emotionally easy one, and part of Cassie wanted to crawl into bed, turn off the lights, and sob, but she was equally grateful to have someone there who wouldn't let her do that.

Cassie hung her coat on the hook in the kitchen, poured herself a cup of coffee from the pot Tilly had evidently made for them to share, and sat down across from her friend. She'd called Tilly when she'd decided to stay in New York, but hadn't spoken to her since Patrice's funeral.

Tilly took a moment to study Cassie. "So, where is he?"

Cassie sipped her coffee before answering. She attempted to gather her strength to answer the first of what was likely only the beginning of a long list of questions from Tilly. "He's in New York with his brothers."

"When is he coming here?"

After letting out a long, shaky sigh, Cassie said, "I don't know if he is."

Tilly pushed a tray of brownies toward Cassie. "Chocolate always helps."

Cassie smiled sadly and bit into one. Her eyes rounded. "Did you make these? They're amazing."

Tilly didn't look as impressed. "Annabelle Sable made them. She asked me to ask you if she can continue working here even though you're back."

Cassie took another bite and savored the taste. "I wish I could afford to hire someone. These are fantastic."

Tilly wrinkled her nose. "I don't believe you'd have to pay her. She and the others had a hen party here every day. Honestly, I don't know how I survived it. I stayed over at Myron's house so I could have some peace in the mornings."

Cassie choked on her coffee. "You stayed over at Myron's house? Did the two of you . . . I mean . . . you didn't . . .?"

Tilly rolled her eyes. "Have sex? You can say the word, Cassie. You won't shock me. I lost my virginity back when you were no more than a twinkle in an angel's eye."

"So? Did you?"

A small smile curled Tilly's lips. "We did."

"And?"

Tilly's cheeks turned pink. "Viagra is a beautiful thing. Now eat another brownie. You look thinner than when you left. And don't think you can change the subject. What happened with Luke?"

Cassie took another square but instead of eating it, she broke it into small pieces on her plate. "It was tough, Tilly. Hard to wait for him and harder to leave without him."

"Then why did you?"

"He asked me to. He said he needed time to sort some things out."

Tilly nodded slowly. "Did he go to his mother's funeral?"

Cassie's mind filled with images of that day while she continued to tear apart the brownie. "He did. He stood in a receiving line next to his brothers. It was beautiful and sad at the same time. She wasn't a nice woman, but somehow she brought four amazing men into the world. I can't begin to tell you how kind Luke's brothers were to me during the days that led up to her funeral. No one knew if Luke would even come back for it. I should have felt out of place, but everyone was so warm and welcoming. I think the funeral helped Luke appreciate his family more. The line of relatives was out the door and never ending. It was odd to see that many people show up for a woman not many seemed to care for."

Tilly laid a hand on Cassie's. "No one goes to a funeral for the dead."

Except me, Cassie thought. *I went for you, Emma.* Cassie held Tilly's hand in hers. *And I don't regret one moment of the journey you sent me on. I'm not afraid of being alone anymore, Emma. Because I see now that I'm not. I'll have a baby someday, maybe with that man, maybe on my own, but it won't be my only family.*

As if on cue, a sharp knock on the door disrupted them, followed by Bonnie sticking her head in and saying, "Oh, good, you're back. Tilly, you were supposed to call me when she got in."

Tilly smiled. "At my age, who can remember anything?"

Bonnie laughed and joined them at the table. "Don't you try to pull that 'I'm too old' crap on me. Your mind is as sharp as a tack. You just wanted to be the first to get the scoop."

"Maybe," Tilly acknowledged with a shameless shrug.

"So, what did I miss?" Bonnie asked.

Cassie caught her up quickly. When she finished, Bonnie sat back in her chair, folded her arms across her chest, and pursed her lips in frustration. "I was sure he loved you."

Cassie studied the last sip of coffee in her cup. "I think he does, but sometimes that's not enough."

"Bullshit," Tilly said harshly.

Cassie and Bonnie both sat up straighter at her tone.

Tilly continued, "Do you want me to speak to him? I'll tell him no matter how beautiful his face is, no one is going to care as long as his head is stuck that far up his ass."

Cassie was the first to burst out laughing. Bonnie quickly followed suit. They laughed so long tears were running down their cheeks. Tilly gave in and started laughing, also.

Tilly's son walked into the kitchen and looked at the three women in hysterics around the table. He picked up one of the brownies and sniffed it. "Mom, it's getting late. You should come home."

Unable to stop laughing, Tilly said, "Cassie, Jimmy thinks you're feeding me funny brownies."

"Funny?" Bonnie asked.

"You know, the illegal type." She turned to her son and said, "You worry too much, Jimmy. There's nothing in these brownies, but even if there was, I'm eighty. All drugs should be legal after a certain age as a reward for making it this far."

"I'll be in the car," her son said with a frown.

Bonnie held her next burst of laughter until after Jimmy was out of the house. "Tilly, how did someone like you have someone like him?"

Cassie chimed in, "Hey, he loves you. He just thinks I'm a bad influence on you. Wait until he hears about you and Myron. He's really going to hate me."

Bonnie leaned forward. "Myron? As in 'I've wanted you my whole life, Tilly' Myron? You finally slept with him and didn't even tell me? Tilly, how could you?"

Tilly adjusted the front of her blouse modestly. "I have a reputation to protect. So don't let it get beyond this kitchen." She studied her freshly painted nails. "Now which one of you wants to go outside and tell my son to go on home because I'm sleeping at Myron's tonight?"

The three ladies started laughing again until they were gasping for air. Cassie thought about Luke and how much she wanted him with her, but she didn't feel the need to hide and cry anymore.

She was home.

And, with or without Luke, she was going to be okay.

✧　✧　✧

A FEW DAYS later, Luke sat with his three brothers at a table in Richard's posh, uptown restaurant. The food was phenomenal as usual, but Luke was too distracted to appreciate it.

Midway through the meal, Luke laid his fork down on

the table and said, "I asked you all to meet me here because I want to announce a few decisions I've made."

Nick's eyebrows rose comically and he looked back and forth between the serious expressions on Gio's and Max's faces. "I bet I can guess them. I'm really good at this."

Gio took a swig of his drink and said, "Let Luke speak, Nick."

Max lent his support to Nick. "Do we have to pretend to be surprised?"

Some of Luke's tension about speaking to his brothers dissolved. There would likely always be a layer of sarcasm in their banter with each other, but lately it was said humorously and not defensively. "I'm leaving New York," Luke said. "I've handed in my resignation at the hospital and have started the process to get licensed in Ohio."

"Shocking," Nick said dryly.

Gio laid a hand flat on the table. "Don't forget you agreed to one Sunday dinner a month at Uncle Alessandro's home. I'm not going without you."

Max laughed. "I think all the children running around makes Gio nervous."

"I'll fly back for it," Luke said, finding it easier and easier to smile.

Gio waved a thumb at Nick. "Nick has this crazy idea that we're having a triple wedding in the fall. I don't know how he did it, but the women are excited about it now. You need to be part of that, also."

Luke tapped his fingers on the table beside his plate. "I don't want to be part of a triple wedding." A strained silence fell over the table. Luke continued, "It needs to be a quadruple wedding or nothing."

It took a moment for his brothers to get what he'd said then a general laugh erupted from them.

"Congratulations," Max said, and clapped a hand on Luke's back.

"That was one of my guesses," Nick said with a self-satisfied smile.

"Did you ask her yet?" Gio watched Luke's face closely.

Luke's eyes shifted uncomfortably beneath the scrutiny. "I bought the ring."

Nick burst out laughing. "You're announcing you're marrying a woman you didn't propose to yet?"

Luke raised a hand in defense. "I didn't take out an ad in the newspaper. You're the first people I've told."

Max brought a hand to his forehead. "Have you spoken to Cassie since you sent her back to Ohio?"

Luke frowned. "No, but I told her I would go to her after I cleared up a few things here."

Richard appeared at the table in his chef whites. "How is everything tonight?"

Nick joked. "Fantastic. Luke announced he's getting married. He decided to join our wedding-fest. The only problem is he hasn't asked Cassie yet."

Richard's lips pressed together as he tried not to smile. "It's customary to do it in the reverse order, but Luke has a good plan I'm sure."

"I am closing up my apartment here in the city. I resigned from the hospital and will soon be licensed to practice medicine in Ohio. Everything is set."

"And the proposal? What of that?" Richard asked.

Not sure what Richard meant, Luke said again, "I bought a ring."

"Mon Dieu," Richard said and spoke to himself for a moment in French. "If you don't do better than that, I will never hear the end of it from Maddy." He snapped his fingers. "Have I ever asked you for anything, Luke?"

"No."

"But I have always been there for you whenever you needed something, yes?"

Luke answered cautiously, "Yes."

"Please ask my wife to help you plan this proposal. She has been so sad since the funeral, and she thinks you're still upset with her. Maddy is good with things like this, and it would mean a lot to me if you included her somehow."

Luke sighed. "If Maddy gets involved, the whole Andrade clan will show up." As he said the words, he thought about what Cassie had said she yearned for more than anything else. Family. He said slowly, "The whole Andrade clan. Richard, you're a genius."

Chapter Twenty

A S SOON AS Cassie received a package from a courier, she threw on her coat, stuffed the envelope in her pocket, drove over to pick up Tilly, and called Bonnie at her restaurant to tell her they were on their way.

Within moments she and her two closest friends were huddled at the end of the restaurant counter. Cassie laid the unopened card down between them.

Bonnie picked it up and inspected it. "Are you sure it's from Luke?"

"It has to be," Cassie said. "It came with three dozen red roses."

Tilly grabbed it from Bonnie and handed it back to Cassie. "The only way to really know is to open it."

Cassie held her breath and hugged the card to her chest. "This could be his way of saying thank you, but goodbye."

Tilly waved a hand in the air. "Suspense is wasted on people my age. I don't want to be dead by the time you figure out if Luke has come to his senses. Open the damn card."

Cassie tore it open. "It's an invitation with directions for how to RSVP."

Bonnie chewed her bottom lip. "He's inviting you somewhere. That has to be good news."

Cassie turned the card so her friends could read it. "He's inviting us."

"Us?" Bonnie and Tilly asked in unison.

Cassie read over the invitation again. "It says I'm invited to an Andrade family gathering on Slater Island this coming weekend. I can bring as many guests as I wish as long as I call this number and tell them how many. Everyone should bring at least an overnight bag and be prepared to spend the weekend." Cassie took out her phone. "He disappears, and then this? I should tell him where he can shove it."

Bonnie snatched her phone from her. "Oh, no you don't. This is his big romantic apology. It could be where he proposes to you. Don't kill the romance by calling him."

Cassie looked to Tilly for her opinion.

Tilly nodded in agreement. "Telling him off might feel good, but is it what you want to do? The problem with your generation, Cassie, is that you often choose instant gratification and cheat yourselves out of what would have been better if you'd had a little patience."

Confused and afraid to believe in anything as good as what seemed to be happening, Cassie asked, "What if it's not an apology or a proposal? What if this is a fundraiser or something he invites everyone to?"

Tilly raised one eyebrow and said seriously, "If that's the case, we take him aside and beat the tar out of him. Then we come home and have a toast to the most clueless man on the planet."

Not too much was scary when Tilly broke it down that way. Cassie smiled, hopped up and down with joy, and waved the invitation. "I'm going to an Andrade weekend."

"We," Bonnie corrected with a whoop of joy. "There is no way you're going without me. Can I bring Greg? We don't close up our restaurant often, but this will be the vacation we could never afford. I've been reading online about the Andrades. I can only imagine what kind of party they would have. Please say yes."

"The invitation says I can bring as many as I'd like, so that means yes to your husband. Tilly, are you in? Do you want to bring your son?"

"Jimmy?" Tilly snorted. "Not if we intend to have any fun. I might bring Myron, though."

Bonnie chuckled. "Ooh, Tilly has a boyfriend."

"We were going to take it slow, but—"

Cassie finished for her, "At your age, who has time?"

All three of them burst out laughing.

Tilly said, "Exactly."

Cassie called the number on the card and spoke to a woman who sounded as if she were someone's secretary. It was all very business-like, even though Cassie felt giddy as she told the woman she was RSVP'ing for five. Two couples and herself.

"That's fantastic, Ms. Daiver. If you give me everyone's address, I will have a limo pick you and your guests up on Saturday afternoon." Cassie did and the woman continued, "You'll be flying out of Toledo on a private plane so there are no luggage restrictions. Mr. Andrade has arranged a selection of services you may choose from for the days leading up to your departure. Would you like me to list them?"

Cassie put the woman on speakerphone and motioned for Tilly and Bonnie to lean in. "She wants to know what we want to do before we go."

The woman described a day that started with visiting a famous spa in Grand Rapids then shopping at a variety of designer dress shops in Perrysburg. "Or we could have everything come to you if you prefer."

Silently, Bonnie mouthed, "Oh, my God."

"This is too much," Cassie said. "We can't say yes to this."

Tilly looked less impressed. She whispered, "I respect that Luke doesn't flaunt his money, but let the man try to impress you this once."

"Yes," Bonnie clapped in excitement. "Please let him try to impress us . . . I mean you." She laughed. "Come on, things like this don't happen here. I am going to enjoy every moment of this right along with you."

Cassie mulled it over. She didn't want Luke to think his money played any part in how she felt about him. For that reason, saying no might be better. On the other hand, he'd taken his time deciding how he wanted their relationship to move forward. They'd been on an emotional rollercoaster with a particularly bumpy ride the last couple of weeks. If this was his way of apologizing and showing her he cared, maybe Tilly was right, and she should let him put some effort into it.

Later, she could explain to him she didn't need anything so fancy. But for now, she and her two best friends were saying yes to a day of pampering and a weekend away.

Everything else would work out however it was supposed to. Cassie was beginning to trust that most things did.

✧   ✧   ✧

LUKE FLEW TO Slater Island on Friday afternoon. He stopped in his tracks when he entered the previously barren foyer. Now filled with furniture, no less than a hundred people were gathered in the adjoining rooms. Many were staff Maddy had said were essential to such an event. They were greeting arriving guests and walking around with trays of food and beverages. Among the elegantly dressed adults, a herd of children darted, laughing over some prank they had pulled on one of their cousins.

Maddy had called the entire Andrade clan together—for him. Luke was touched beyond words by her thoughtful extravagance. He'd never distanced himself from his cousins so the chaotic nature of how they gathered was nothing new to him, but he hoped it wouldn't be too much for Cassie.

Uncle Alessandro saw Luke and came over to greet him with a bear hug. "We needed this. I'm proud of you, Luke. What a perfect way to introduce Cassie to the family."

Luke hugged his uncle back then said, "If it doesn't send her running."

Alessandro didn't look worried. "Gio, Nick, and Max are all coming?"

Luke nodded. "Yes. They think it makes sense to test

drive the island's ability to handle all of us before we start planning the weddings here."

Alessandro moved his hands in the air expressively. "It will be the perfect location. Max chose well when he bought homes here. The locals have been incredibly welcoming." When Victor walked into the foyer, Alessandro waved him over. As he approached, Alessandro said softly, "Talk to your uncle. He's worried that what you heard changed something between you." As soon as Victor joined them, Alessandro excused himself and walked away.

Victor's eyebrows furrowed as if he were carefully choosing his first words. "Luke, I'm sorry that you had to—"

Luke interrupted him with a warm pat on the arm. "I know, Uncle Victor."

"I wish I could go back in time and—"

Luke stopped him with a raised hand. "You don't need to say it. I put the past to rest with my mother."

Victor raised his chin. "I knew you would forgive me. Your father was the same. Be proud of that. He was a good man with a big heart. He chose the wrong woman to give it to, but I've met your Cassie, and she's the type of woman who will appreciate your loyalty and the love you have for her. Your father would be pleased with your choice."

Luke cleared his throat. "Let's just hope she says yes."

Victor laughed. "If not, we do this again and again until she does."

Luke smiled. "You would, wouldn't you?" His uncle didn't have to answer. They both knew he was serious. Well, Cassie wanted a family. Luke hoped she was ready to be part of one that was as large as it was crazy.

Speaking of crazy, Luke spotted Maddy giving instructions to one of the house staff. He couldn't help but smile. For as much as she drove him nuts, Maddy had poured herself into making sure the weekend would be perfect. He snuck up behind her and gave her a big hug.

"You're here," she exclaimed and gave him a kiss on the cheek. "Everything is coming together. Don't go in the kitchen. Richard is having a fit because I didn't order the right pans for whatever he had planned for dessert tonight. I tried, but he knows I don't cook. He'll get what he needs delivered. Just save yourself, and avoid him until he works it out."

Luke laughed. Richard was mild-mannered everywhere except in the kitchen and yet there, outside of his wife and kids, was where he said he found the most joy. "Duly noted."

Maddy raised one hand in a request for Luke to wait, walked a few feet away, picked up a small package, then rushed back. "This weekend will fly by, especially once Cassie arrives. I have something I want to give you." She handed him what felt like a notebook wrapped in tan paper.

"What is it?" Luke started to open it.

Maddy stopped him. "Not now. Put it aside, and open it when you get back to Ohio."

Luke's hand tightened on the package. "Tell me it's not the journal you tried to give me before. What could possibly be in it that I would want to read?"

Maddy raised her shoulders in apology. "I debated giving it to you or burning it, but I couldn't help feeling it belonged with you. Throw it away if you want, but I didn't feel it was my place to make that decision."

Luke tossed it on the table behind him. "Thank you, I guess."

Maddy opened her mouth then snapped it shut as if reconsidering what she was going to say. Luke sighed impatiently. "What? You might as well say it."

"I tried to invite Gigi this weekend, but she wouldn't take the call from me."

Luke placed his hands in his trouser pockets and rolled back on his heels. "That's not a surprise. She won't talk to any of us."

Maddy made a face. "It makes me so sad to see her house sit empty this weekend while all of yours are filled with family. Don't give up hope. She doesn't want to be here only because she doesn't know us. But she will one day. Who knows, maybe she will by the time you all have your weddings here."

Luke looked down at his forever-hopeful cousin. "That would be nice, wouldn't it?"

"Anything can happen as long as you don't give up hope."

Luke bent and gave Maddy a kiss on the forehead. "Don't change, Maddy."

She gave him an impish smile. "I don't intend to."

Chapter Twenty-One

CASSIE STEPPED OUT of the island taxi van that had driven her, Tilly, and Bonnie—and their men—from the airport to Luke's home. Beneath her long winter coat, she was wearing a midnight-blue dress that had been tailored to hug her curves perfectly. She was determined to wow Luke without shocking his family. Bonnie had helped her choose appropriate, but sexy thong panties.

The wind off the ocean was cold on her bare legs, but she didn't care. The sun was shining brightly, and people were gathered on the lawn as well as the porch of not only Luke's home, but also the homes surrounding it.

Cassie's chest tightened. She turned to Bonnie who was standing at her side. "Look at all the people, Bonnie. This isn't a family gathering. What do you think this is?"

Bonnie pointed to the homes around Luke's. "Could it be some sort of block party? Those three houses are also decked out for a celebration."

Clutching her purse to her side, Cassie said, "If I'm right, each one of these homes belongs to one of Luke's brothers. His youngest brother, Max, bought them so they would have a place for their family to gather."

"They needed four mansions to do that?" Bonnie asked.

"Five," Cassie corrected. She looked to the final home on that stretch of the island. "I bet that house is for Luke's half-sister."

"It looks empty. What happened? Did they forget to invite her?" Tilly asked gruffly.

Cassie hugged an arm to her stomach as another cold ocean breeze blew across her bare legs. "It's a long story and not mine to tell, but they're estranged. Max bought the house, but Gigi has never seen it. It's just sort of there, waiting for her if she decides to have a relationship with her brothers."

"That's so sad," Bonnie said, then joked to lighten the mood. "I wonder if they're looking to adopt more siblings? If so, we're completely available," she turned to her husband, "aren't we, Greg?"

He hugged her from behind. "I don't need a big house to make me happy. I already have everything I need right here."

Bonnie turned her head and gave him a warm kiss. "You always did know exactly what to say."

He chuckled. "But it must be nice to live like this."

Tilly clucked. "If there's one thing I've learned in my life it's to not envy anyone. Everyone has their trials. I doubt the people in that house are any happier than we are."

Myron took her hand in his and brought it to his lips. "They couldn't be."

Tilly blushed. "You old flirt."

Cassie loved that her two friends were with men who

made them smile, but it also filled her with an ache she couldn't deny. She wanted that with Luke, but the more she looked around, the more convinced she was that Luke's invitation had been an act of kindness rather than one of romance. *This isn't the setting for a proposal. Maybe this is Luke's way of thanking me for being there for him while his mother was very ill. I hope this isn't how he says goodbye.* "I'm glad Luke let me bring friends with me. I would have been nervous going in there alone."

"You won't be alone," Bonnie said as she pointed to the door.

The front door of the large house they had pulled up to opened, and Luke stood in the doorway. He was dressed in a dark suit and looked completely at ease despite the chaos around him. He walked purposefully down the large stone steps toward them, never taking his eyes off her.

He stopped just in front of her and smiled. "I've missed you, Cupcake."

She wanted to say, "You didn't have to," but she kept that thought to herself. Instead, she said, "Your invitation said I could bring friends. I hope you don't mind that I did."

"I couldn't imagine today happening without them." Luke beamed his warm smile at her friends. He shook hands with Greg and Myron then hugged Tilly and Bonnie. "Let's go inside where it's warmer." He put a hand on Cassie's back and guided her toward the house.

Their progress was slow. Every few feet they were stopped by a member of Luke's family. Cassie had held her breath during the first introduction, curious as to how he would refer to her. When he said, "This is Cassie Daiver and her friends," Cassie's heart had sunk.

He didn't say, "This is my girlfriend."

Not, "This is the woman I told you about."

No, he kept everything so formal that Cassie couldn't help but become discouraged. She told herself not to be. What was he supposed to say? *This is Cassie, a woman I thought I loved while I was sad about my mother being ill. She's a good person, though, so I brought her here to thank her.*

She didn't allow herself to think about what she wished he would say. She told herself it was enough he'd made this effort to ensure she understood she was special to him. As more and more introductions were made, Cassie gave up trying to remember the names of his cousins and began to simply smile at everyone. It wasn't likely she'd ever meet them again, anyway.

As Luke guided Cassie toward the house, he told himself to breathe. When he'd seen her standing almost shyly beside the taxi, he'd wanted to run down the stairs, pick her up in his arms, and carry her off to the nearest bedroom. He'd wanted to kiss her, but he knew if he did he wouldn't be able to stop. He didn't want to lose his head to passion. He wanted her to have the proposal Maddy said women spoke about for the rest of their lives, and that didn't include a mauling on the lawn in front of her friends and his family.

When they entered the foyer of his home, Cassie shed her coat, and Luke's calm scattered to the wind. Her dark blue dress hugged her form intimately, clinging to each curve he could remember the feel of too well. She smiled up at him as if waiting for him to make a comment, and he tried to, but when their eyes met all he could think about was how much he loved her and what a fool he had been for almost losing her.

A firm slap to one of his shoulders brought Luke back to the present. "Are you going to let the poor girl into the party or keep her to yourself in the hall?"

Cassie smiled and didn't seem surprised by the hug Uncle Alessandro gave her. "It's wonderful to see you again. Alessandro, these are my friends, Bonnie and Greg, Tilly and Myron."

Alessandro shook everyone's hand warmly. "It's a pleasure to meet your friends. We're so happy you were able to join us for this big day."

Without missing a beat, Cassie asked, "What exactly is your family celebrating?"

Alessandro shot Luke a questionable look. "Luke didn't say?"

Cassie turned to Luke, but he looked away. It wasn't as if he could have told her. Should he have told her? She had to know on some level this was about her. If she didn't think this was for her, what did she think he'd invited her to? "She just arrived, Uncle Alessandro. We haven't had time to talk. I thought I'd let her settle in, meet some of the family."

Alessandro raised both hands in deference to Luke's preference. "However the night unfolds, it will be one to remember, no?" He turned toward the party and checked his watch. "It's later than I thought. Maddy gave me strict instructions to have you both in the side ballroom by six. Don't be late."

"Us both?" Cassie repeated in confusion.

Luke nodded. "We'll be there."

Gio and Julia walked over as soon as Luke brought Cassie into the open area of the foyer. Gio formally introduced himself and his fiancée to Cassie's friends, but his expression warmed when he greeted Cassie. "Julia misses having you around, Cassie."

Julia nudged him with her elbow and leaned toward Cassie as if speaking in confidence. "He misses you, too. He was saying that just this morning." She turned to Bonnie and Tilly, and with a huge, warm smile, said, "I've heard so much about both of you. When things settle down, come find us. I'd love to get to know you better."

Just like that, Cassie's friends relaxed and Luke could have hugged Julia for—well, for being herself. That feeling passed, however, a moment later when Julia took both of Cassie's hands in her and exclaimed, "Everyone is here, even some Andrades I've never met. Aren't you excited?"

Cassie's eyes rounded nervously. "Should I be?"

Julia looked at Luke's face and quickly said, "Oh. Oh. No. I meant, isn't it fun to meet so many new people?"

Gio shook his head wryly, but his lips were stretched as if he were fighting a smile.

Luke met Bonnie's eyes. By her expression, she had guessed what was going on, but he shook his head ever so slightly, hoping she would get the message. She did, or at least seemed to since she didn't say anything.

Tilly watched the exchange closely. Luke would have bet money she also knew exactly what was going on. He wondered again if he should warn Cassie about what he had planned, then remembered what Maddy had said about how that would remove the magic from the moment. This was for Cassie, and he wanted it to be perfect. "We're making our way to the ballroom."

"So are we," Gio said, as if it were a coincidence.

When Luke placed his hand on Cassie's lower back and began to usher her toward the ballroom, she resisted and said, "Ballroom? Luke, I don't dance."

He leaned down and whispered in her ear, "Tonight you do."

Chapter Twenty-Two

LUKE'S HUSKY COMMENT had sounded like a dare, and Cassie had found the idea sexy until she actually walked into the ballroom with him. She wanted to be held in his arms even if it were only on a dance floor and only for a night. The room he led her into, though, was full of couples spinning each other around in a colorful, sophisticated circle. The perfection of how the couples moved through the space to the soft, instrumental music almost seemed choreographed.

Cassie dug her heels in and brought Luke to a halt beside her. "I can't do that."

He smiled, took her hand, and pulled her through the couples until they were near the middle of the room. "I'll guide you," he said and spun her around him.

Cassie looked to her friends for help, but they were both in the arms of the men they'd come with and joining the other couples, having fun even if they weren't doing all the steps correctly. Cassie tripped over Luke's foot, and her cheeks flooded with warmth. She probably couldn't have shown him more clearly why she didn't belong on the dance floor with him, or in this life for that matter. She tried to pull away from him. "I told you I don't dance."

He stopped and took her face between both of his hands. "That's because I've been a poor partner. The waltz, Cassie, is about trust. You trusted me, and I let you down. I know I need to earn that trust back, and I will, Cupcake. I'll do whatever it takes to prove to you I meant it when I said I loved you."

Cassie searched his face. The love she'd seen in his eyes before was back tenfold and it brought tears to her eyes. "You've been through a lot, Luke. I understand."

"No, I don't think you do," he said, and kissed her lightly on the lips.

He reached into his coat pocket and dropped down to one knee. It was only then Cassie realized they were alone on the dance floor with everyone watching them from the sides. He opened a ring box and held it up to Cassie. "Marry me, Cassie. Let me spend the rest of my life showing you why we belong together."

Cassie swallowed hard and looked around the room again. She wanted to believe it was actually happening, but the whole scene felt like a dream, and she didn't want the heartbreak of saying yes then hearing her alarm clock sound. The more she looked around, the more nervous she became as she realized everyone was waiting to hear her answer.

Luke stood and put a hand beneath Cassie's chin, bringing her face around to his again. "Cassie, this is about us, not them."

"Then why are they here?" Cassie asked breathlessly. She

couldn't help it. She'd never been in front of so many people. Her stomach was twisting nervously, and she was pretty sure she was about to throw up any minute.

Luke held her eyes. "They're here because they love me, and they know I love you. They're family, Cassie. My enormous, crazy family. Yours too, if you'll have me. Say something. If you don't agree to marry me soon, some of them are going to pass out from holding their breath. You took a leap of faith and followed me to New York. Believe in me, one more time. Say you'll spend the rest of your life with me because I don't want to imagine spending one day without you."

Cassie looked around again. "Do you really think I fit into this world? I'm happiest in my kitchen covered with flour. I don't belong here."

"I'm happiest when I'm in your kitchen with you. I don't care where we live as long as it's together. Do you love me?" he asked and every last one of Cassie's doubts disappeared.

"Yes," she answered.

"Then trust me, Cassie. I won't let you down again."

From across the perfectly silent room, Tilly called out, "If you don't marry him, I will."

Cassie laughed at that and said, "That settles it then. Before she snaps you up, Luke, I will marry you. I don't want to imagine another day without you either."

He slid a diamond ring onto the fourth finger of her left hand and pulled her to him for a deep kiss. The room exploded with cheers, but Cassie didn't feel self-conscious anymore. She was with Luke, and that was all that mattered.

Music began to play again, this time a vaguely familiar tune. Luke raised his hands for her to take and asked, "May I have this dance?"

Cassie smiled up at him and winked. "You may have every dance."

As Luke moved, Cassie moved with him, and her confidence grew. He was right, it all came down to trust and even though Luke had asked for time to sort through his mother's loss, he had always been honest with her. The man who was twirling her around this fancy ballroom was the same man who had frosted cupcakes with her and taken her to meet his friends. "I love you," she burst out.

He kissed her deeply before twirling her around him again. "And I love you, Cassie Daiver, my adorable cupcake, so much more than you know."

Cassie heard the words of the music playing and asked, "Is this a Disney song?"

With a grin, Luke said, "Maddy helped me plan this evening. Sounds like she's poking a little fun at me, but I don't mind. I was wrong, and lately, I was a bit of a beast."

"Don't change too much. Every woman I know was a little disappointed at the end of that movie. The beast was sexy."

"Really?" Luke growled in Cassie's ear. "We'll have to revisit this topic tonight when we're alone."

Feeling light as air as he spun her again, Cassie laughed. "If you want to spend the night talking, sure. It wasn't what I imagined we'd be doing, but whatever."

✧ ✧ ✧

THE NEXT MORNING Luke woke early and, for a long time, watched Cassie sleep beside him. Once they were alone, Cassie hadn't held it against him that he'd sent her home to Ohio alone. She'd understood and accepted him as she always had. He thought he knew what love was until she'd come into his life and given herself to him: Passionately. Completely. Unconditionally.

At the beginning of the evening she'd seen only the extravagance of the evening and worried she didn't belong, but as more and more of his family had expressed their gratitude that Luke had found someone like her, she had begun to relax. The Andrades were everything his mother had always accused them of being: loud, boisterous, and flamboyant. But they were also big-hearted, loyal, and accepting of each other. They fought, but they made up because to an Andrade, family was everything.

Luke looked down at Cassie.

He understood the term family better now than he ever had. His started with Cassie. It encompassed three sometimes-frustrating brothers he couldn't imagine his life without, and countless cousins and uncles who had always been there for him.

It was with that sense of inner peace he found the strength to slip away from Cassie, get dressed, and head downstairs in search of the package Maddy had given him. The house was blissfully empty. It should have been in shambles after the number of people who had been there the night before, but he'd never again doubt Maddy's ability to mobilize an army of staff.

Luke found the wrapped notebook exactly where he had tossed it. He picked it up and carried it into the living room. With the notebook still in hand, he sat in a chair before the unlit fireplace and debated what to do with it.

If the journal held more secrets than his mother had spat at Victor, Luke was sure he didn't want to know them. Gio would never read it. Nick might, but Luke didn't want him to. Beneath Nick's façade of humor, was a man who had once turned to alcohol to numb the emotional wounds their mother had inflicted on him. Luke wouldn't do anything to send Nick back to that. And Max? Max would tell him to burn it. And maybe he'd be right.

"You're up early. Are you okay?" Cassie asked from behind him as she slid a gentle hand over his shoulder and down his chest. She kissed the side of his neck.

He tossed the notebook on the table beside him and took her by the hand, pulling her around the chair and into his lap. "I am now." He kissed her deeply, loving that he could start every morning with the taste of her lips on his.

She laid a hand on his cheek when their kiss ended. "What are you doing down here?"

Luke sighed, picked up the book from the table, and handed it to her. "Maddy gave me this."

"What is it?"

"It's my mother's journal."

"Oh."

"Exactly."

"What are you going to do with it?"

"I don't know. Even when I had to face what my mother had done to my family, I still thought she'd show remorse at the end. She didn't, Cassie. She was poisoned, but in the end it was the anger in her that was too much for her heart to take. Ironic, isn't it, that I covered up something that was potentially not even the reason for her death?"

Cassie turned the wrapped notebook in her hands, studying it. "How do you think Maddy got it?"

Luke shrugged. "I'm sure I don't want to know."

"Were you getting ready to burn it?"

"I was considering it."

Cassie held it out to give it back to him. "It's yours now. You should do that if it'll make you feel better."

Luke didn't take the journal back. "There couldn't be anything in it worth keeping, could there?"

Cassie looked at Luke for a long moment then tore off the wrapping paper. "There's only one way to find out." She flipped the journal upside down and shook it. Nothing came out. She smiled sheepishly. "Sorry. Maybe I've watched too many movies. I was hoping something would fall out."

Luke took the book back from her and was preparing to throw it in the fireplace when he saw something. "Is it odd that the back of the journal is thicker than the front?"

Cassie smiled. "Now you're thinking like me. Does it look like you could peel it off?"

Luke flipped the notebook on its side and pulled at a

corner of the back cover. When it came off, a piece of paper fell out.

"Holy shit," Cassie said.

"Indeed," Luke said. He dropped the journal to the floor beside him and scanned the first paper. "It's my father's will. He left Isola Santos to Gio and the rest of his estate was to be divided up between his five children. Why would the will be in my mother's journal?"

"Did Gigi get anything when your father died?"

With growing understanding, Luke shook his head in shock. "No, everything went to my mother. No one even questioned it. My mother came from a wealthy family. She didn't need his money. My brothers and I have trust funds from our grandparents."

"Looks like you need to talk to your sister."

"My sister," Luke said sadly, "won't even take my call."

Cassie kissed him softly on the lips. "From what I know about Andrades, they don't hear the word no."

"Is that a complaint?" he growled.

"I wouldn't change one damn thing about you, Luke Andrade. Take that will and go find your sister."

Luke stood up and flipped Cassie over one of his shoulders. He slapped her ass playfully and said, "After we put a little more work into making that baby you want."

Cassie laughed and squirmed even though they both knew she wasn't trying to get away. "What are you doing, Luke?"

Still carrying Cassie over his shoulder, Luke took the

stairs up to his bedroom two at a time.

"I'm going to ravish you completely, as any good beast would."

Epilogue

A MONTH LATER Cassie was seated in the enormous kitchen of Uncle Alessando's house with several women from the family. Although the women were wearing expensive dresses, they were cuddling young babies and bouncing toddlers on their laps. When Luke had first explained how he wanted both of them to return to New York once a month for a family dinner, Cassie hadn't known what to expect. She was beginning to understand that Andrade gatherings were never small, a fact that made her love them even more.

Growing up, Cassie had often dreamed of one day having a large family. With the Andrades, she felt like she'd won the relative jackpot. Looking around at the women who had welcomed her so warmly into their group, Cassie smiled. When she'd been invited to arrive early to help, she'd readily agreed, but she should have guessed it wouldn't involve any actual cooking. It appeared that the only one allowed to cook on Sundays in the Andrade home was Maddy's husband, Richard, and his kitchen staff.

With her youngest son on her hip, Maddy stood and said, "I would like to call this meeting to order.

"Meeting?" Tara, Max's fiancée asked quickly. She turned to look at Cassie for confirmation that she wasn't alone in being lost.

I've got nothing, Cassie mouthed silently.

"First," Maddy continued, "there is the matter of the bet."

"The bet?" It was Cassie's turn to parrot in confusion.

A beautiful, dark haired woman Cassie had met once before, who was, if Cassie remembered correctly, married to Luke's cousin, Stephan, said, "Maddy, you do realize that when you talk like this in front of new people we always sound a little crazy."

Maddy smiled. "Nicole, we are a little crazy."

Rena, Nick's fiancée, laughed out loud and leaned toward Tara and Cassie. "They are. They really are."

Maddy waved a hand in the air as she returned to her agenda. "Abby couldn't be here today because she and Dominic are traveling, but she gave me permission to speak for her and the other two teams are represented. We need to either pick a winner, void the bet, or double down."

Julia turned to Cassie. "We should explain better. It took me a little while to understand, and I'm on a team. Tara. Cassie. Your soon-to-be family and some of their best friends were worried that Gio, Nick, Luke, and Max were disconnected from the family. The ladies decided the best way to mend the rift was to play matchmaker. They broke into teams and each tried to find the perfect woman for their cousins. The first team to successfully orchestrate the most engagements would win the title of best matchmaker in the family."

Surprised, but somehow not, Cassie asked slowly, "So, who chose you, Julia?"

Julia chuckled. "I was working as a security officer at Gio's company. I don't count."

Rena tapped a hand on the table. "I've known Nick most of my life. I don't count, either."

Tara folded her arms over her chest as she absorbed the story. "Hang on. Maddy, did you hire me as part of a matchmaking bet?"

Maddy shook her head quickly. "Oh, no. I never pictured you and Max together." She blushed. "I didn't mean that the way it sounded. I meant, because you're so . . ."

Nicole laid a hand on Maddy's arm. "Stop. You're digging yourself deeper."

Maddy sighed. "I adore Tara. She's perfect for Max. I just didn't realize he had good taste in women."

Rena chuckled. "Good save, Maddy."

"Can I count her as my team's win? I mean, I did find her."

"No," the group said in unison.

"So that leaves only Cassie." Maddy turned a critical eye on her. "I did fly out to Ohio to meet her."

Rena countered, "But she and Luke were already together by then."

"I also planned their engagement party," Maddy added and turned to Cassie for support. "Cassie, all you have to do is say the beautiful event I put so much time into planning was the reason you agreed to marry Luke."

Rena leaned over the table and put a hand on Cassie's. "Don't let her pressure you, Cassie. You can tell her you would have said yes even without the party."

Cassie looked around the table and noted the expectant expressions. "If I say the engagement party was the clincher, the bet is over?"

"Yes," Maddy said quickly.

"What happens if I say it wasn't?"

Rena raised a hand. "We could double down. There is still Gigi. From what I hear, she's single."

Maddy's eyebrows shot up and she asked in surprise, "You want our bet to continue?"

Rena shrugged with humor. "I hate to lose as much as the next person."

Tara sat up straighter. "Gigi, Max's sister, right? The one they've all been trying to get in touch with? How would you play matchmaker with her?"

Julia smiled. "Every team has their secrets. You want in?"

Tara nodded.

Julia turned to Cassie. "How about you?"

Cassie hedged. "I'm not sure how Luke would feel about me being involved in this."

Rena rolled her eyes. "Are you kidding? If Luke were a woman he'd be on Maddy's team. All he'll care about is if we succeed."

Maddy waved her hands in excitement. "I already have an idea, too. But I'm not saying anything."

"Okay, I'm in," Cassie said. "Which team will I be on?"

"To be fair, we should put Tara in Abby's group. That

way there is one person with security background on each team."

Rena said, "Then I claim Cassie. You're with me. Have you met Abby's sister, Lil?"

Cassie blushed. She'd met so many people recently. "I think so."

"How about Alethea? Tall gorgeous woman with red hair?"

Tara interjected, "Do not let her near your phone."

"My phone?" Cassie asked. "I don't know what you're talking about."

Tara scanned the room. "I'll explain later. She may be listening."

Maddy laughed. "Tara, you are so dramatic. The things you say. Alethea is one of Dominic Corisi's security, and she is sometimes over the top when it comes to surveillance, but she wouldn't have any of us bugged." Maddy paused, seemed to think about it more, then asked, "Would she? Hey, Alethea, if you're listening, Cassie's on your team."

Julia waved a hand. "We also need to discuss our weddings. Are we moving forward with a quadruple ceremony?"

Tara's eyes rounded. "That's a big wedding."

Rena nodded. "An Andrade wedding is huge regardless. I'm okay with it. I like the idea of Nick and his brothers sharing that special day."

Julia took Rena's hand in hers. "Gio gets all choked up about it every time I mention it. And I'll be happy to have a set date. You already feel like my family; let's do it."

They all turned to Cassie.

"I'm in," Cassie said without hesitation. "Are we still planning on using Slater Island?"

Tara wiped a tear from the corner of her eye. "Do you know how much it will mean to Max if we do that?"

Rena added, "Nick, too. Those homes were the best gifts Max could have given his brothers. They have something concrete that binds them together."

"Gio feels the same way," Julia added.

"Luke, too," Cassie said, loving these women more each time they spoke. She had told Luke she wanted to wait before making any announcements, but she was so moved by the emotion in the room, she blurted, "As we talk about dates, you all need to know I'm pregnant and due next winter. Can we choose a summer or early fall date?"

With a huge smile, Julia said, "Congratulations. And, of course, we'll work the date around that. I'm so happy for you."

Maddy leaned forward, hugged her with her free arm, and asked in excitement, "And it's Luke's?"

A hush fell over the room.

Nicole admonished her softly, "Maddy."

Maddy went three shades of red and started to say something, but Cassie cut her off. Maddy had kept her secret while it mattered. That's what mattered. "It's Luke's."

A tear ran down Maddy's face. "I'm so happy."

Cassie's smile grew, and she wiped an emotional tear from her own cheek. "We're pretty damn happy ourselves."

"Just promise me one thing," Maddy said earnestly.

Cassie answered easily, "Anything."

"Let me plan the baby shower. I'll keep it simple."

Rena sat back in her chair and said dryly, "Which means at least two hundred people."

Two hundred people? Cassie gulped.

Maddy defended herself with humor. "We can't invite the American cousins without inviting our Italian ones. You don't do that to family."

"Family," Cassie said softly and laid her hand on her still flat stomach.

Emma, I found my family. Here and back in Defiance.

I don't know how much of this you did or if you can even hear me, but—thank you.

THE END

Acknowledgements

I am so grateful to everyone who was part of the process of creating *Somewhere Along the Way*.

Thank you to:

Nicole Sanders at Trevino Creative Graphic Design for my cover. You are amazing!

My very patient beta readers. You know who you are. Thank you for kicking my butt when I need it.

My editors: Karen Lawson, Janet Hitchcock, and Marion Archer.

Melanie Hanna and her amazing husband, for helping me organize the business side of publishing.

My Roadies for both their friendship and their feedback.

Dr. Carol Dubois and her husband, Dr. David Dubois, for help with medical terminology and the logistics of what Luke could do for an accident victim.

Kathleen Dubois being a promotion wonder!

My husband, Tony. Couldn't do this without you.

My children for laughing with me instead of getting upset when I burn dinner while answering emails.

My niece, Danielle Stewart, and my sister, Jeannette Winters, for joining me in self-publishing and brainstorming with me along the way. *Always better together.*

About the Author

Ruth Cardello was born the youngest of 11 children in a small city in southern Massachusetts. She spent her young adult years moving as far away as she could from her large extended family. She lived in Boston, Paris, Orlando, New York—then came full circle and moved back to New England. She now happily lives one town over from the one she was born in. For her, family trumped the warmer weather and international scene.

She was an educator for 20 years, the last 11 as a kindergarten teacher. When her school district began cutting jobs, Ruth turned a serious eye toward her second love– writing and has never been happier. When she's not writing, you can find her chasing her children around her small farm, riding her horses, or connecting with her readers online.

Contact Ruth:

Website: RuthCardello.com
Email: Ruthcardello@gmail.com
FaceBook: Author Ruth Cardello
Twitter: @RuthieCardello